HEARTS IN THE SNOW

(The Miracle Creek Amish Romances, Book 3)

GRACE SPRINGFIELD

An Amish Romance Novel

ISBN 978-1-918219-23-4

First Edition: 2025
Published by: Cosmic Jive Publishing

www.cosmicjivepublishing.com

For permissions and inquiries, contact:
info@cosmicjivepublishing.com

Disclaimer:

This is a work of fiction. Names, characters, businesses, places, events, locales, and incidents are either the products of the author's imagination or used in a fictitious manner. Any resemblance to actual persons, living or dead, or actual events is purely coincidental.

Chapter 1
Winter's Return

The predawn darkness still clung to Miracle Creek when Emma Mast lit the first lamp in the bakery. Her breath fogged in the cold air as she measured flour, the familiar rhythm steadying her hands. Cinnamon and cloves scented the room—Christmas spices that had filled this space for three generations.

Outside, snow blanketed the town in peaceful white. The bakery stood on Main Street, its windows soon glowing warm against the winter cold. Emma had arrived an hour before dawn, as she did every day, to prepare the breads and pastries that would fill the display cases by the time the first customers arrived.

"Did you see Mrs. Graber's new buggy?" Joanna flitted past with a tray of cooling racks, her *kapp* strings bouncing. "Sky blue! Can you imagine? *Datt* says it's too showy, but I think it's beautiful."

Emma smiled but kept her focus on the dough. Her younger sister could talk through a thunderstorm, her enthusiasm for life's small dramas inexhaustible. The *lebkuchen* cookies needed Emma's full attention—traditional recipes their grandmother had taught her, though she'd added her own touches over the years. A hint more ginger here, a touch of orange zest there. Small rebellions that felt both thrilling and dangerous in a community that valued tradition above innovation.

"Everyone says your *lebkuchen* are the most delicious in all of Lancaster County!" Joanna leaned against the counter, flour dusting her dark dress. "You should make those peppermint cookies for the market. I could help sell them! We'd make a fortune."

Emma's hands stilled on the rolling pin. The peppermint bread had been her secret project for months now, something new mixed with the old. She'd experimented with the recipe late in the evening, after the bakery closed and Joanna had gone home. The combination of traditional spices with fresh peppermint created something unique, something that honored the past while reaching toward the future. But tradition mattered in their community. Perhaps too much.

"Perhaps," she murmured, pressing the star-shaped cutter into the dough. Each cookie emerged perfect, yet she couldn't shake the feeling that perfection itself had become a kind of cage. She'd been making the same cookies, the same breads, the same pies for years now. The customers loved them, relied on them. But sometimes Emma felt like she was baking herself into a corner, becoming as predictable as the seasons.

The bakery door creaked open, bringing a gust of winter wind and her father. Michael Mast stamped snow from his boots, his weathered face stern in the lamplight. He'd been up since four, tending to the animals and checking the livestock before coming to help with the market preparations.

"*Gut* morning, *Datt.*" Emma wiped flour from her hands, noting the lines of fatigue around his eyes. He worked too hard, had done so ever since her mother's illness last winter.

"Cold out there. Temperature dropped overnight." He set a heavy bag on the counter, ice crystals still clinging to the canvas. "Brought the last of the apples from the root cellar. Let's review what we need for the market booth."

Emma nodded, listening as he ticked off their usual items—sourdough, cinnamon rolls, the traditional pies that had been family recipes for generations. All safe choices. All proven sellers. The list could have been written ten years ago, twenty years ago. Nothing changed in Miracle Creek, not if the elders had their way. Change meant risk, and risk meant potential loss of the carefully maintained order that kept their community strong.

"What about the peppermint bread?" She tried to keep her voice light, casual, as if the question didn't matter much. "I've been perfecting the recipe. The test batches have been popular."

Michael's brow furrowed as he examined the small loaf she offered, turning it in his work-roughened hands. He broke off a piece, chewing thoughtfully. Emma held her breath, waiting for his judgment. Her father's approval meant everything—not just for the business, which she ran in all but name, but for her sense of place in their world.

"We've always done well with what we know, Emma." His voice was measured, careful. "It honors our past, but..." He paused, considering his words. "Change brings risk. The bakery feeds our family. Helps employ others. One failed experiment could damage everything we've built."

"I used our traditional techniques," she pressed, hearing the desperation creep into her voice despite her efforts to sound reasonable. "The base is the same recipe *Mammi* taught me. I just added something fresh, something that might draw in the younger crowd. The tourists especially would love something new."

"Perhaps we focus on established favorites first." He set the loaf down gently, not meeting her eyes. "We wouldn't want to risk losing the trust of our patrons. Trust is hard to build and easy to lose."

Emma's fingers pressed into the dough she was kneading, working out the frustration she couldn't voice. She understood his caution. She even agreed with it, mostly. The bakery had supported their family through lean years and good. It was more than just a business—it was a web of responsibility and relationships that couldn't be risked lightly.

But the flame of ambition flickered stubbornly in her chest, refusing to be snuffed out by practicality. She wanted to create, to innovate, to leave her own mark on the tradition she'd inherited. Was that pride? Was that the worldly ambition that Bishop Lapp warned against? Emma couldn't tell anymore where healthy aspiration ended and sinful pride began.

They worked in companionable silence for the next hour, the rhythm of their tasks as familiar as breathing. Michael rolled out pie crusts while Emma shaped loaves and Joanna decorated cookies with practiced efficiency. The bakery came alive around them, warmth spreading from the ovens, yeasty smells filling every corner. This was what Emma loved—the alchemy of flour and water and heat becoming something nourishing, something beautiful.

As the sun lifted over the horizon, casting the snow-covered street in soft hues of pink and gold, the day's first customers began to arrive. Mary Beiler, the Elder's wife, stopped in for her daily loaf to feed her ever-growing family. Daniel Troyer followed, picking up six cinnamon rolls for his construction crew. Then came young Hannah Andrews, spending the last of her pocket money on a pastry before school—her ginger braids, tied with faded ribbons, looking somehow brighter each time Emma saw her. Finally, a group of *Englisch* tourists wandered in from the bed-and-breakfast down the street, marveling at every detail, snapping photos, and asking endless questions about Amish traditions. Emma answered each one with patient courtesy, though she firmly refused when they tried to take her picture.

"Oh my gosh, she's so beautiful!" exclaimed one gray-haired tourist, her holiday-themed sweatshirt stretched tight across her middle. "You're just adorable, honey!" She turned to her husband—who was wearing a matching, equally snug sweater—and lowered her voice only slightly, as if Emma couldn't hear. "Such a waste, all that beauty hidden under a frumpy dress and *kapp*. Look at that hair! Those eyes!"

"Like Purdah," her husband muttered absently, more interested in the pastries than the conversation.

Emma lowered her gaze to the counter, cheeks warming, and said nothing. She was used to such comments—well-meaning, but ignorant. It wasn't a waste. And it certainly wasn't Purdah. It was tradition—one she chose to honor. A beautiful, meaningful tradition. Yes, it could feel confining at times—like any small-town life, she supposed—but she would still take that over the noise and restlessness of the *Englisch* world.

She looked up, looked the tourist full in the eye. She guessed they meant well. "Will there be anything else?"

By mid-morning, the rush had eased. Michael had gone back to the farm, leaving Emma and Joanna to handle the slower afternoon trade. Emma used the quiet to tidy up, scrubbing flour from the wooden counters worn smooth by generations of hands.

Meanwhile, Joanna amused herself by imitating the tourist from earlier, putting on an exaggerated Boston accent. "Oh my gosh, you're so beautiful, honey!" she cried, collapsing into laughter before reaching out to gently brush a stray lock of blonde hair from Emma's face.

Her tone softened. "You really are beautiful," she whispered. "Inside and out. Don't ever forget that."

Emma's cheeks colored again. She ducked her head, uncomfortable with praise, and murmured, "Ach, Joanna..." Then, after a small pause, she smiled and added softly, "So are you, *schwester.*"

As evening fell and the last customers left, Emma stepped onto the back porch of the bakery, needing air, needing space to think. Snow blanketed the town square in peaceful white, lanterns glowing in shop windows like fallen stars. Beautiful. Familiar. Sometimes suffocating.

She breathed in the cold air, watching her breath cloud. The blacksmith's forge glowed across the way, John Hostleter still at work despite the late hour. The Kings' general store's lanterns also blazed. Each building held stories—births and deaths, courtships and weddings, arguments and reconciliations. The whole town was a tapestry of interconnected lives, each thread dependent on the others.

Somewhere beyond these streets, beyond the careful boundaries of their life, other possibilities waited. Emma had seen them in the faces of *Englisch* tourists, heard them in their stories of cities and universities and careers. But standing here, looking at the home she loved, she couldn't quite imagine what choosing those possibilities would mean. Leaving would break her father's heart, disappoint the women who worked there part-time and depended on the bakery for income, unravel the careful place she'd made for herself in this community.

And yet. And yet the peppermint bread sat on the counter inside, a small act of defiance wrapped in flour and sugar. A promise to herself that she wouldn't completely disappear into tradition, that somewhere inside the dutiful daughter and reliable baker, Emma Mast still had dreams of her own.

The wind picked up, bitter against her face. Emma pulled her shawl tighter and went back inside, locking the door behind her, already planning tomorrow's baking schedule. The same breads. The same cookies. The same life.

But tucked in the back of her mind, that flame still flickered.

* * *

The bus wheezed to a stop at Miracle Creek's edge just as full dark settled over the town. Noah Albrecht stepped down into the winter evening, his breath fogging as he surveyed the town he'd left five years ago. The simple Amish clothes he'd changed into at the last rest stop felt foreign against his skin after so long in English attire—the rough homespun scratching where cotton and polyester had once glided smooth.

He gripped his worn satchel tighter, feeling the weight of the few possessions he'd brought back with him. Five years compressed into a single bag. Five years of trying to make himself fit into the *Englisch* world, of construction jobs and night shifts and city apartments that never felt like home. Five years of running from something he could never quite escape.

The town looked frozen in time—pine garlands on storefronts, lantern light in frosted windows, the distant sound of children's laughter echoing off snow-packed streets. But he had changed. The scar on his cheek proved that much. Three inches of puckered skin, a souvenir from a bar fight in Columbus that he'd never meant to be part of. He'd been trying to help a woman being harassed, had gotten a broken bottle across the face for his trouble. The *Englisch doktors* had stitched him up, but the scar remained—a visible mark of the violence and chaos he'd encountered in the wider world.

"Evening, Noah!" Esther Coblenz called out from her porch, her smile uncertain, not quite reaching her eyes. The aged widow held a broom, had probably been sweeping snow from her steps when she spotted him.

He nodded politely and kept walking, boots crunching in the packed snow. Whispers followed him like shadows. The prodigal son returns. He could almost hear their thoughts, feel their judgment pressing against his back like a physical weight. Five years was long enough to become a stranger. Long enough to become a cautionary tale told to young people tempted by the world beyond Miracle Creek's borders.

At the general store, warm light spilled from the windows. Noah pushed open the door, a bell jingling overhead. Albert King was restocking shelves, his broad shoulders and salt-and-pepper hair exactly as Noah remembered. Some things, at least, remained constant.

"Ach, well I never! Noah Albrecht!" Albert's eyes widened, then crinkled with genuine warmth. "Didn't expect to see you back in these parts. Heard you were in Ohio, or was it Pennsylvania now?"

They shook hands, and Noah felt the weight of unspoken questions in the older man's grip. Albert had always been direct, never one for dancing around difficult topics. It was one of the things Noah had always appreciated about him.

"Ohio for a while. Then other places." Noah set his satchel down, flexing fingers stiff from the cold. "How have you been?"

"Can't complain. Business is steady." Albert studied Noah's face, his gaze lingering on the scar. "How was it? Out there in the *Englisch* world?"

"Different." Noah spoke carefully, weighing each word, conscious of the other customers in the store. In the corner, Veronica Zook pretended to study a bolt of fabric, though her posture made it clear she was listening as intently as ever. Some things in Miracle Creek never changed. "Very different from here," he finished quietly.

"Your father's been managing the farm alone." Albert's tone held gentle reproach. "Harvest was hard this year. We all felt it. Lost some crops to early frost, and the prices weren't what we hoped."

The guilt Noah had been carrying settled heavier on his shoulders. His father wasn't young anymore. Running a farm alone was brutally hard work, especially as Gideon Albrecht approached sixty. Noah should have been there, should have been helping, should have stayed instead of running away five years ago.

"I heard," Noah said quietly. "That's part of why I came back."

"Planning to stay awhile this time?" The question was casual, but Noah heard the deeper inquiry beneath it. Could they count on him? Or would he run again when things got difficult?

"For the season. Then we'll see." The words came out automatically, a shield against commitment. Against hope. Against the possibility of failing again.

Albert adjusted the brim of his hat, his weathered eyes studying Noah—the same eyes that had watched him grow from a lanky boy into a man still searching for where he fit in the world. "People will have their suspicions about why you're back," he said after a moment. His voice dropped lower still, cautious, as he noticed Veronica Zook inching ever closer while pretending to inspect a spool of thread. "And you should know… there's been talk about Emma Mast."

Noah's chest tightened at her name. *Emma.* He'd tried not to think about her during his years away, had tried to convince himself that whatever they'd had was a childish infatuation best left in the past. It hadn't worked. Her face still appeared in his dreams, her laughter still echoed in his memories.

"What kind of talk?" His voice came out rougher than intended.

"Isaiah Weaver's been courting her. Well—trying to," Albert said, reaching for a jar of preserves to restock the shelf, his movements deliberate. "Bishop Weaver's son, you know, from over in Hope Valley. Everyone says it'd be a *gut* match. Solid family, *gut* prospects. Emma hasn't given him an answer yet, though. Been stalling him for months, or so folks say."

The words landed in Noah's chest like a blow. He had no right to feel anything—no right at all. He was the one who'd left her, without a word or a reason, disappearing like smoke on a cold morning. Of course she'd moved on. What else could she do? What else should she do?

"I see," he said finally, the words rough in his throat.

And yet—despite the guilt that twisted inside him—he couldn't stop the flicker of relief that followed. She hadn't married. Not yet.

"Isaiah's a *gut* man," Albert continued, his tone carefully neutral. "Maybe a bit rigid in his thinking, but devoted to the community. Bishop Lapp is encouraging the match. Emma's father seems agreeable to it."

Everyone had decided Emma's future except Emma herself, Noah thought. But that was how things worked here. Marriage was as much about joining families and strengthening community bonds as it was about love. He'd forgotten that during his time away, forgotten how little individual desire mattered against the weight of collective expectation.

Albert and Noah lingered a few more minutes, exchanging small talk—weather, crops, and the latest news from around town. When it was time, Noah paid for the winter carnations he'd picked out for his mother, slung his satchel over his shoulder, and stepped back into the crisp air. The cold bit at his cheeks, but it was Albert's words about Emma that lingered, echoing relentlessly in his mind as he walked.

The walk to his family's farm took twenty minutes through the snow. Noah used the time to prepare himself, to shore up the walls he'd need to get through whatever reception awaited. The white farmhouse appeared through the trees, smoke curling from the chimney— home, or the memory of it. The barn stood solid and dark, the fields beyond covered in snow. Everything looked exactly as he remembered, as if time had stopped the moment he'd left.

He paused at the gate, steeling himself. His hand trembled slightly as he reached for the latch. This was it.

Five years of absence, five years of silence, all coming to a head in the next few minutes.

The front door flew open before he could knock. His mother's dish clattered to the floor, forgotten, shattering on the worn wooden boards.

"Noah!" Miriam Albrecht's voice broke as she rushed to embrace him, not caring about the broken dish, not caring about the cold air flooding into the house. She smelled of bread and lavender soap, exactly as he remembered. Her arms wrapped around him with fierce strength, and he felt five years of loneliness crack open in his chest. "Oh, my boy, you're finally home!"

"I'm home, *Mamm.*" His voice was rough with emotion, muffled against her warmth, his throat tight with tears he refused to shed.

She pulled back to look at him, her hands cupping his face, her eyes searching his features as if memorizing them. Her fingers traced the scar on his cheek, her expression pained. "What happened to you out there?"

"It's nothing. An accident. It's healed now."

But his father stood back by the corner post, arms crossed. Gideon Albrecht's face was weathered as old oak, carved by years of hard work and hard weather. His expression was unreadable in the shadows, but Noah felt the weight of his judgment, his disappointment, his anger at being abandoned.

"You've been away a long time, Noah," his father said finally. Each word measured, weighed, found wanting. "Five years. Not a letter. Not a word except that one phone message through Albert saying you were alive."

"I know. I'm here now."

"*Gut.*" Not forgiveness, not yet. But not rejection either. It was more than Noah had dared hope for.

His sister Bethany appeared in the kitchen doorway, her eyes wide. At fifteen, she'd grown from the little girl he remembered into a young woman on the cusp of adulthood. Another reminder of all he'd missed, all he'd thrown away.

"Noah!" She squealed and threw herself at him, all teenage exuberance. "You're really back! I thought you were gone forever!"

"Not forever, Bethany." He hugged her, feeling her trembling. "Just for a while."

"Five years is forever," she said, pulling back to study his face. Her finger traced the scar, her expression troubled. "Did someone hurt you?"

"It's nothing. Don't worry about it."

As they gathered for a simple meal—stew and fresh bread, nothing fancy but filling—Noah felt the weight of his father's silence across the table. Five years of absence sat between them like a stone wall. They spoke of practical things—the farm, the weather, community news. His father explained the challenges of the recent harvest, the struggles with equipment breakdowns, the neighbor who'd helped when Gideon threw out his back in September.

Each detail was a small indictment, a reminder of how his absence had created real hardship. Noah wanted to apologize, to explain, to make them understand why he'd needed to leave. But the words stuck in his throat. How could he explain that staying had felt like suffocating? That the weight of expectations had been crushing him? That he'd needed to find out who he was beyond the role prescribed for him since birth?

Words could only do so much to breach the wall between them. They'd need time, and work, and patience he wasn't sure either of them possessed.

Later, alone in his childhood bedroom, Noah unpacked his satchel. The room was exactly as he'd left it —the same narrow bed with its patchwork quilt, the same wooden dresser his father had built for his tenth birthday, the same view of the barn and fields from the window. Only the dust on the windowsill suggested time had passed at all.

He pulled out a carved chess piece—a king, polished smooth from months of handling. He'd made it during his time away, teaching himself the intricate woodwork in the long evenings after construction shifts. An English coworker had taught him the finer points of carving, techniques that went beyond the basic woodworking skills his father had taught him. The piece blended English craftsmanship with Amish simplicity, neither one nor the other but something in between. Like him.

He set it on the windowsill where moonlight caught its curves, illuminating the careful detail work. A reminder of who he'd been, who he'd become, and the question of who he might still be. The king stood alone, waiting for the rest of the pieces. Waiting for a game that might never be played.

Through the window, he could see the lights of Miracle Creek twinkling in the distance, a constellation of lanterns marking homes and businesses. Somewhere out there, Emma was probably closing up the bakery, or sitting with her family by the fire, or thinking about Isaiah Weaver's proposal. Maybe she was happy. Maybe she'd forgotten all about the promises they'd whispered to each other that last summer before he left.

Or maybe, just maybe, she was thinking about a boy who'd left without saying goodbye, wondering if he'd ever have the courage to come back.

Noah pressed his forehead against the cold glass, his breath fogging the window. He tried to pray, searching for the words that would make sense of his tangled feelings, his confusion, his hope and fear all mixed together. But the prayers wouldn't come. They'd stopped coming somewhere in Ohio, in some anonymous apartment where he'd felt more alone than he ever had in Miracle Creek.

Gott felt distant, unreachable. Or maybe Noah had wandered too far to find his way back.

He undressed in the dark, climbed into the narrow bed, and stared at the ceiling. Tomorrow he'd start working on the farm, would begin the long process of proving himself to his father, to the community. Tomorrow, he'd face the whispers and the judgment and the careful distance people would maintain until they decided whether he was truly back or just passing through again.

Tomorrow he might see Emma.

The thought filled him with equal parts longing and dread. What would he say to her? How could he explain five years of silence? What right did he have to feel anything when he'd been the one to leave, the one to break whatever fragile thing they'd had?

Sleep was long in coming. When it finally arrived, Noah dreamed of summer afternoons and a girl's laughter, of promises made under the stars, of a life he'd thrown away in search of something he'd never quite found.

Chapter 2
Unexpected Encounter

Emma pushed open the door to Albert's General Store the day after Noah's return, the bell jingling overhead with its familiar cheerful sound. She needed fabric for the Christmas quilt—something festive but not too bold. The annual charity auction required each family to contribute, and Emma had volunteered to make a quilt this year.

The bolts of cloth lined the walls in the muted colors preferred by their community—burgundy and forest green, hunter's plaid and cream, deep blue and soft gray. No bright reds or vivid purples, nothing that would draw attention or suggest pride. Emma ran her fingers over the fabric, feeling the textures, imagining patterns.

"Did you hear about Noah Albrecht?" Dorcas Hershberger's whisper carried across the store, sharp as a needle piercing fabric.

Emma's fingers froze on a bolt of cranberry fabric, her heart stuttering in her chest.

"He's back," Veronica Zook confirmed, her voice rich with the satisfaction of sharing important news. "Changed, they say. Has a scar now, right across his cheek. Saw plenty in the *Englisch* world, I imagine. Who knows what he got up to out there. You know how those *Englisch* cities are—full of sin, pride and temptation."

Emma's pulse quickened, her breath shallow. Noah. After five years of silence, five years of wondering, five years of telling herself she'd moved on. Her hand trembled as she reached for another bolt of fabric, trying to appear casual, unaffected, as if her world hadn't just tilted on its axis.

"I heard he's staying at his father's farm," Veronica continued. "Poor Gideon Albrecht, trying to run that place alone all these years. My husband says the fields aren't what they used to be. Can't manage everything yourself at that age."

"Well, Noah abandoned them once," Dorcas said, her tone judgmental. "Who's to say he won't do it again? Some people just aren't made for our life. Always wanting more, never satisfied with Gott's provision."

Emma wanted to defend him, wanted to say that they didn't know the full story, that there were reasons for everything even if those reasons remained hidden to her. But her throat was tight, words trapped behind the careful facade she'd constructed over five years of pretending not to care.

Her elbow knocked into the jar display.

She grabbed for it, but too late—glass shattered across the floor, sticky preserves spreading in a sweet, humiliating puddle. Strawberry and peach mingled with shards that caught the lamplight like scattered jewels, like the broken pieces of her carefully maintained composure.

"Ach nee!" Emma dropped to her knees, face burning. Of course this would happen. Of course she'd make a spectacle of herself the moment Noah's name was mentioned, proving to everyone watching that she wasn't as unaffected as she pretended to be.

"It's alright, dear!" Dorcas hurried over with a broom quickly gotten from Albert, her expression knowing. "Just a bit of fruit. Happens all the time."

But it didn't happen all the time. It happened now, when Emma's careful control had shattered as surely as the glass, when her carefully constructed indifference lay exposed as the lie it was.

Her hands shook as she picked up larger pieces, carefully avoiding the sharp edges.

"Here, let me help," Veronica said, bringing a dustpan, again proffered by Albert. She worked alongside Emma, but her eyes held speculation, as if she'd just confirmed something she'd suspected.

As they cleaned, Emma's thoughts raced, tumbling over each other like water over stones. Noah, here in Miracle Creek. The boy—no, the man now—who had once been her whole world. The one who'd left without saying goodbye, without explanation, vanishing like morning fog burned off by the sun. She'd been seventeen, convinced that what they had was real and lasting. And then one morning he was simply gone, with only a brief note left for his parents saying he needed to see the world beyond Miracle Creek.

She'd waited months for a letter, for any word. Nothing came. Eventually she'd accepted that he wasn't coming back, that whatever promises they'd whispered beneath the stars meant nothing against his need to escape.

The bell jingled.

And in that moment, Noah stepped inside, and time stuttered. Their eyes met across the aisle—his brown and warm, still familiar after all these years despite the changes.

Five years collapsed into a heartbeat. He looked different—broader shoulders from physical labor, harder lines around his eyes that spoke of difficult experiences, that scar cutting across his left cheek like a brand. But his gaze held the same intensity that had once made her feel like the only person in the world.

For a moment, neither of them moved. Emma was dimly aware that she was still kneeling on the floor surrounded by broken glass and spilled preserves, that Veronica and Dorcas had stopped cleaning to watch this reunion with avid interest, that her blonde hair was probably coming loose from her *kapp* and her apron was stained with strawberry. She'd never felt more exposed, more vulnerable.

"*Gut* morning, Emma," Noah said cautiously, as if weighing the sound of her name on his tongue, uncertain how it would be received. "Ladies..." He gave a brief nod to the others, but his eyes quickly returned to Emma, lingering a moment longer than polite.

"Welcome back, Noah." Her voice came out steadier than she felt, though her hands shook as she pressed them against her apron, trying to hide the trembling.

They both reached for the same fallen jar, perhaps instinctively trying to do something normal, something that would break the strange spell of their reunion. Their fingers brushed—a spark that shot through her like lightning, electric and dangerous and familiar.

She pulled back as if burned, her heart hammering against her ribs so hard she thought he must be able to hear it.

"Seems we both have some catching up to do," Noah said with a half-smile that didn't quite reach his eyes, didn't quite bridge the distance between them.

"*Ja*, it seems so."

They made awkward small talk while Veronica and Dorcas continued cleaning but remained close enough to hear every word. The weather—colder than usual for December. Town changes—the new kerosene lamps in the meetinghouse, the Stoltzfus family's bright red hay wagon that everyone was talking about. Old Hezekiah's passing last spring, a loss that had touched the whole community. Safe topics that kept them from saying anything real, anything that mattered.

But Emma felt the weight of everything unsaid pressing against her chest, heavy as stones. *Where were you? Why didn't you write? Did you think about me at all? Do you have any idea how much it hurt to be left behind without explanation?*

Behind her, she could feel Veronica's eyes boring into her back, memorizing every word, every gesture, every fleeting expression. By tonight, half the community would know about this encounter, the story growing with each retelling until it bore little resemblance to reality.

Emma gathered her fabric quickly, suddenly desperate to escape, to get away from Noah's presence and the memories it stirred up, away from the watching eyes and speculative whispers.

"I should go. Take care, Noah."

"See you, Emma."

Outside, she gulped cold air like a drowning woman breaking the surface. Her hands shook as she clutched the fabric to her chest, walking fast toward the bakery. Five years she'd convinced herself she was over him. Five seconds of eye contact proved her a liar.

The snow crunched under her boots as she hurried down Main Street, passing the blacksmith's shop and the furniture maker's, the familiar landmarks of her circumscribed world. But everything looked different now, as if Noah's return had tilted reality slightly off-kilter.

Back at the bakery, Emma found Joanna arranging fresh cookies in the display case, humming a hymn from Sunday service. Their younger brother, Thomas, hovered nearby, eagerly "beta-testing" the treats—not that they needed it.

"You're back quick," Joanna said, then froze when she saw Emma's face. "What's wrong? You look like you've seen a ghost."

"Noah Albrecht is back." The words fell flat, factual, failing to convey the storm of emotions churning inside her.

Joanna's eyes widened. "Noah? After all this time? Did you see him?"

"Who's Noah–?" Thomas began, but both sisters cut him off with a quick shush.

"At the general store. We spoke briefly."

"What did he say? How does he look? Is he staying?" Joanna's questions tumbled out in her usual whirlwind of curiosity.

Thomas persisted. "Who's Noah?"

Emma set down the fabric she had been holding and moved behind the counter, needing something to do with her hands. She began wiping down surfaces that were already spotless. "It doesn't matter. It was a long time ago. We were children."

"You're only twenty-two now," Joanna pointed out. "But you weren't children when he left. You were seventeen—practically promised to each other, from what I remember. *Datt* was furious when Noah left."

"Was Thomas Emma's… boyfriend?" Thomas asked innocently, eyes wide. He had only been three at the time.

Joanna waved him off with the practiced motion sisters reserve for annoying little brothers, then turned back to Emma.

Emma swallowed hard, remembering the months after Noah's disappearance—her father forbidding her to speak his name, the compounded pain of losing him, and the sting of his disappointment for allowing herself to care for someone so unreliable.

"That's in the past," Emma said firmly, both to reassure Joanna and herself. "Isaiah Weaver has asked Father's permission to court me. Bishop Lapp approves. It's a *gut* match."

"But… do you love Isaiah?"

The question hung in the air. Emma's hands moved over the counter, scrubbing at an imaginary spot, avoiding Joanna's gaze. "Love isn't everything," she said quickly. "Respect and compatibility matter more in a marriage. Isaiah is steady, reliable, devoted to the community. He'd be a *gut* husband."

Her words tumbled out in a rush, as if saying them fast enough might silence the doubt gnawing at her own heart.

"That's not an answer," Joanna said softly, her voice gentle but insistent.

No, it wasn't. Because the truth was Emma didn't love Isaiah, didn't feel her heart race when he appeared, didn't lie awake thinking about him. She respected him, appreciated his many good qualities, could imagine a calm and stable life as his wife. But there was no spark, no passion, no sense of coming alive when he was near.

Not like with Noah.

The thought was dangerous, disloyal. Emma pushed it away and returned to scrubbing the counter.

"We should finish preparing for tomorrow's market," she said, changing the subject with obvious intent. "The Christmas season is our busiest time."

Joanna accepted the deflection, moving on to talk about other things—gossip about neighbors, plans for the holiday market, speculation about whether it would snow again before Christmas. Emma made appropriate responses, but her mind was elsewhere, caught in the past, tangled in memories she'd tried so hard to bury.

That evening, after the bakery closed and Joanna had gone home with Thomas, Emma stood at the window watching snow fall through the lamplight. The town looked peaceful, serene, like a scene painted on glass. But inside her chest, chaos reigned.

Noah was back. That simple fact changed everything, turned her carefully ordered world upside down. She'd made peace with his absence, had convinced herself she was content with the life planned out before her. Marriage to Isaiah. Children. A quiet existence devoted to family and community. It was a good life, the life she was supposed to want.

But seeing Noah again had cracked something open inside her, had reminded her of dreams she'd buried, of the girl she'd been before learning to be practical, cautious, careful. That girl had believed in romance, in passion, in love that transcended duty and expectation. That girl had whispered promises under the stars and believed they'd last forever.

That girl was a fool.

Emma locked up the bakery and walked home through the winter night, her footsteps muffled by snow. The day after tomorrow - Sunday - she'd see Isaiah at church. Then she'd smile and be pleasant and give him every reason to believe his courtship was progressing well. Then she'd be the practical, sensible woman everyone expected her to be.

But tonight, alone in the darkness, she let herself remember. Summer afternoons by the creek. Stolen moments in the barn. The way Noah's hand had felt in hers, warm and sure. The promises they'd made, the future they'd imagined.

All gone now. All impossible.

The snow fell heavier, covering her tracks, erasing the evidence of her path. By morning, it would be as if she'd never passed this way at all.

Chapter 3
Whispers of the Past

Noah hammered shingles onto the barn roof two days after his return, his father working silently beside him. The cold December air bit at his exposed skin, but the physical labor felt good after years of softer English work. This was honest work, the kind that showed results, that mattered.

The rhythm should have been comfortable—they'd done this work together countless times before he left. But now each nail felt weighted with five years of absence, each swing of the hammer punctuated by questions neither man knew how to ask. The silence between them had texture, density, as if words had solidified into something physical.

"Pass me another shingle," Gideon said, his voice gruff.

Noah handed it over, their fingers barely touching. Even that small contact felt loaded with meaning, with the ghost of easier times when they'd worked together and laughed together and understood each other without needing words. Before Noah had become a disappointment, a problem, a son who couldn't be content with the good life he'd been given.

"What was it like?" His father's voice was measured, careful, as if he wasn't sure he wanted to hear the answer but needed to ask anyway. "Out there?"

Noah chose his words like picking through broken

glass, trying to find the pieces that wouldn't cut. "Different. I worked construction for a while. Big buildings, nothing like this. Skyscrapers in Columbus that took months to complete. Got lost in a shopping mall once—that was something. Took me an hour to find the exit. Place was like a maze."

The corner of Gideon's mouth twitched. Almost a smile. It was more than Noah had hoped for, a crack in the wall between them.

"Emma's done well with the bakery," his father said after a long pause, positioning another shingle with exacting precision, not meeting Noah's eyes. "Expanded her offerings. People come from three towns over now. She's got a *gut* head for business, that one. Smart with numbers, knows how to manage employees."

Noah's hammer paused mid-swing. Of course they'd talk about Emma eventually. Of course his father would probe that wound, whether deliberately or not.

"That's *gut* to hear," Noah said carefully.

"She's had suitors. Isaiah Weaver's been persistent. The bishop's son from Hope Valley." Saying it as if his son hadn't already heard it, Gideon positioned the shingle with the same precision he applied to everything, his movements deliberate. "*Gut* match for her. Stable. Respectable. Comes from a strong family line."

The unspoken words hung between them like ice crystals in the cold air: Unlike you. Unlike someone who ran away. Unlike someone who can't be trusted to stay.

The name landed like a blow to Noah's chest, stealing his breath. Isaiah—solid, faithful Isaiah who'd never left, never questioned, never doubted his place in the world. The neighbouring bishop's son, no less, which meant the entire community would approve and support the match.

Everything Noah wasn't anymore. Everything the community wanted for Emma.

"I see." Noah drove the next nail in harder than necessary, the impact jarring his arm, pain shooting up to his shoulder.

They worked in silence as the sun climbed higher, the gap between them feeling wider than before, an unbridgeable chasm opening up. All the questions Noah wanted to ask—Did she ask about me? Did she miss me? Does she ever think about that last summer?—remained locked behind his teeth, impossible to voice without revealing too much, without making himself even more vulnerable than he already felt.

The farm stretched out below them, snow-covered fields that had been in the Albrecht family for four generations. Noah's grandfather had cleared this land, built the original barn. His great-grandfather before that had purchased the property with savings accumulated over years of careful living. This was heritage, legacy, responsibility. And Noah had walked away from it all as if it meant nothing.

"You planning to stay this time?" Gideon asked suddenly, his voice harder now, demanding an answer. "Or are you just passing through again, here until you get restless?"

Noah flinched at the bitterness in his father's voice. "I don't know yet. I came back because—" He stopped, unsure how to finish that sentence. Because I was lonely? Because the *Englisch* world wasn't what I expected? Because I failed out there too? None of those answers would satisfy his *Datt's* need for certainty.

"Because why?" Gideon pressed. "Because you finally remembered you have responsibilities? Because the

Englisch world wasn't as exciting as you thought? Or because you're still running, just in a different direction?"

The words struck like physical blows. Noah set down his hammer, his hands shaking slightly. "I came back because this is home. Because I was wrong to leave the way I did. Because I wanted to—" He struggled to find words adequate to the tangle of emotions inside him. "To make things right."

"Making things right takes more than showing up," Gideon said, his eyes finally meeting Noah's. "It takes commitment. Staying power. Proving you've changed."

"I know that."

"Do you?" His father's gaze was searching, almost desperate. "Because I can't go through this again, Noah. Counting on you, depending on you, only to wake up one morning and find you've disappeared again. Your *mamm* cried for months after you left. Months. I had to watch her grieve like you'd died, except worse because we didn't know where you were or if you were safe."

Guilt crashed over Noah in waves. He'd known his leaving had hurt them, but he'd rationalized it, told himself they'd be better off without him, that his presence was causing more problems than his absence would. He'd been wrong. Selfish. Cruel, even, in his self-absorption.

"I'm sorry," he said, the words inadequate but sincere. "I should have written. Should have stayed in touch. I was wrong about so many things."

Gideon nodded slowly, returning to the work. "Sorry is a start. But it's only a start."

They continued working, the silence now slightly less hostile, slightly more thoughtful. Noah focused on the physical task, the simple satisfaction of nails driven true, of shingles laid straight, of work done properly. This he could control. This he could do right.

By noon, they'd finished one section of the roof. Gideon climbed down the ladder, his movements careful, showing his age. Noah followed, suddenly aware of how much harder this work must be for his father now than it had been five years ago. Another consequence of his absence—his father aging alone, without help, wearing himself down through sheer determination.

"Come inside," Gideon said. "Your mother has dinner ready."

The farmhouse was warm, smelling of beef stew and fresh bread. Miriam fussed over Noah, filling his plate too full, making sure he had the best portions. Bethany chattered about school and her friends, her teenage energy filling the spaces that might otherwise have been awkward.

"Isaiah Weaver came by yesterday," Miriam said, her tone casual but her eyes watchful. "Brought eggs from his mother's chickens. Asked after Emma Mast, wanted to know if I thought she'd enjoy ice skating this weekend."

Noah's fork paused halfway to his mouth. His mother was watching his reaction, he realized. Testing him. Seeing if the mention of Emma and Isaiah together would provoke a response.

"That's nice," he managed, keeping his voice neutral.

"I told him Emma loves skating," Miriam continued. "Remember how she used to skate on the pond every winter? She was so graceful, like a bird in flight."

"I remember." The words came out rougher than intended. He did remember—Emma flying across the ice, her cheeks red from cold, her eyes bright with joy. He remembered holding her hand as they glided together, the world reduced to just the two of them and the endless white expanse of frozen water.

"Isaiah's a *gut* man," Gideon said firmly. "Steady. Devoted to the community. He'll make a *gut* husband for someone."

The message was clear: Emma is moving on. You lost your chance. Don't interfere with something good because of your own selfishness.

Noah ate the rest of his meal in silence, the food tasteless in his mouth despite its obvious quality. After lunch, he excused himself and walked to town, needing to move, to think, to escape the suffocating weight of his family's expectations and disappointments.

The walk took him past the bakery. Through the window, he could see Emma working, her hands moving with practiced efficiency as she kneaded dough. Even from a distance, even through glass, the sight of her made his chest ache. Five years hadn't diminished what he felt —if anything, absence had clarified it, stripped away the confusion of youth to reveal something deeper and more painful.

He forced himself to keep walking, to not stop, to not go inside and complicate her life further with his presence. She deserved stability, deserved Isaiah's steady devotion, deserved better than someone who'd proven he couldn't be counted on.

But his feet slowed despite himself, and before he fully realized it, Noah found himself standing outside Eli Fisher's new woodworking shop—the place his father had said his old friend could usually be found most days and evenings. The small building, tucked behind the schoolhouse, smelled of pine and varnish, sunlight streaming through high windows to highlight Eli's current project: a rocking chair with elegant curves, each line a testament to years of careful craftsmanship.

"Noah!" Eli looked up from his work, a genuine smile spreading across his face. The two men had grown up together. *"Gut* to see you. How's the work at your father's place going?"

"Slow but steady. We're repairing the barn roof." Noah ran his hand over the rocking chair's armrest, appreciating the smooth finish. "Beautiful work."

"Thanks. It's a commission for an English family up in Lancaster. They're willing to pay *gut* money for quality craftsmanship."

Noah gazed around his surroundings. "This used to be Leah Miller's shop!"

"It sure did. She got married a few months ago. To John Hostler's cousin. Went and moved to Tall Poplars so I got myself a sweet deal on the place."

Noah nodded, his face saying that was nice.

Eli set down his tools and wiped his hands on his apron. "How are you settling back in?"

"It's... an adjustment." Noah moved through the shop, examining various projects in different stages of completion—tables with smooth, unbroken surfaces, chairs with intricate carvings, small boxes with hidden compartments. "Everything's the same but different. Or I'm different and everything's the same. I can't tell anymore."

"That's usually how it is when you leave and come back." Eli pulled up two stools, gesturing toward them. "After my *rumspringa*, I was a bit of a mess myself. Have a seat. Tell me what's really on your mind."

Noah hesitated, then decided honesty was easier than pretense, at least with Eli. "Emma. My father mentioned

Isaiah Weaver has been courting her."

"Ah." Eli nodded slowly. "*Ja*, Isaiah's been persistent. Brings her flowers from his mother's hothouse, offers to drive her to market in his buggy, helps with heavy lifting at the bakery. He's doing everything right."

"And Emma?" Noah tried to keep his voice casual. "How does she feel about it?"

"Hard to say. Emma keeps her feelings close. She's pleasant to Isaiah, accepts his help, but..." Eli paused, considering his words. "I don't know. Something seems missing. Folks say Emma looks at Isaiah like he's a business partner, not a potential husband. But maybe that's enough. Not every marriage is about passion. Sometimes steady partnership is better."

The words should have been comforting but instead made Noah's chest tighten. The thought of Emma settling for "steady partnership," of going through life without the spark she deserved, felt wrong. But what right did he have to judge her choices? He'd given up any claim to influence her life when he left without explanation.

"There's been talk about you being back," Eli said, his tone shifting to something more serious. "At the council meetings. Some of the elders are worried. Elder Beiler especially."

"Worried about what?"

"That you might disrupt things. The younger people especially—they see someone who left and came back, and it makes them wonder. Makes them ask questions about whether there's something beyond Miracle Creek worth pursuing." Eli leaned forward. "Noah, I'm your friend, so I'm telling you straight: you need to be careful. The community is watching you. They're waiting to see if you're really back or just passing through. And they're especially watching how you interact with Emma."

"I haven't interacted with her at all, except for running into her at the general store."

"I heard about that!" Eli grinned, shaking his head. Veronica Zook's information network was faster than any army. "That's already more than some people would like. Isaiah's father—the bishop, remember—he has considerable influence. If he thinks you're interfering with his son's courtship..." He spread his hands, emphasizing the unspoken consequences. "Just be careful. That's all I'm saying."

Noah absorbed this information, feeling the invisible walls closing in. He'd returned to Miracle Creek seeking redemption, a fresh start, a chance to reconnect with his roots. Instead, he'd walked into a web of expectations, judgments, and political considerations he'd forgotten existed during his time away.

"I appreciate the warning," he said finally.

They talked for a while longer about neutral topics—woodworking techniques, changes in the community, mutual friends and their families. But the warning lingered in Noah's mind long after he left the shop.

Walking home as evening fell, Noah found himself at the old schoolhouse where he and Emma used to meet during their teenage courtship. The building was closed now, had been for years since the community built a new, larger schoolhouse by Eli's workshop. But the frozen pond beside it remained, its surface smooth and inviting in the moonlight.

He stood at the edge, remembering. Summer afternoons turned to autumn evenings, then winter nights skating under the stars. Emma's hand in his, her laughter echoing across the ice. The promises they'd whispered, the future they'd imagined. All of it felt both incredibly distant and painfully immediate, as if no time had passed at all while simultaneously feeling like a lifetime ago.

"Noah?"

He spun around. Joanna Mast stood on the path, her blue dress bright against the snow, a basket over her arm.

"Joanna. What are you doing out here?"

"Delivering bread to Mrs. Kaufmann—she's been sick and *Mamm* wanted to help." She studied him with the frank curiosity of youth. "What are you doing here?"

"Just walking. Thinking."

"About Emma?" The question was direct, unfiltered by adult caution.

Noah couldn't help but smile slightly at her boldness. "Is it that obvious?"

"Everyone knows you two were close before you left. Everyone's talking about what will happen now that you're back." She shifted her basket to her other arm. "Are you coming to the Christmas singing tomorrow? Emma will be there. She always brings her cinnamon cookies."

"I don't know if that's a *gut* idea."

"Why not? It's a community event. Everyone's invited." Joanna's expression turned sly. "Unless you're afraid to see Emma with Isaiah. He'll probably be there too, making sure everyone sees them together."

The image bothered Noah more than it should. "I'll think about it."

"You should come. It'll be fun, just like old times." She started to leave, then turned back. "Noah? Emma never forgot about you. Just so you know. She tried to, but she never managed it."

Before he could respond, Joanna hurried off into the darkness, leaving Noah alone with thoughts that swirled like the snow beginning to fall.

Emma never forgot about you.

The words echoed in his mind as he made his way home. The farm was dark except for the lamplight in the kitchen window. His mother would be cleaning up after dinner, his father probably already in bed after the long day's work. Bethany would be doing homework or reading by the fire, their black and white Border Collie, Shep, gently snoozing beside her.

Normal family life, the kind Noah had rejected and now desperately wanted back.

But wanting wasn't enough. As Eli had warned and his father had made clear, he needed to prove himself. Show the community he was trustworthy, committed, changed. And part of that meant staying away from Emma, not interfering with the life she was building with Isaiah.

Even if every instinct screamed at him to fight for her, to make her remember what they'd had, to prove he was worth a second chance.

In his room, Noah pulled out the carved chess piece—the king—and examined it in the lamplight. He'd made it as a reminder of what he'd lost, a symbol of the choices he'd made and their consequences. Now it seemed to mock him with its solitary position, its lack of purpose without the other pieces to make a complete set.

On impulse, Noah pulled out his woodworking tools and a fresh block of wood. If he couldn't pursue Emma directly, couldn't interfere with her life, maybe he could find another way to communicate, to remind her of who he'd been, who he might become.

He began to carve.

Chapter 4
The Christmas Singing

The community hall glowed with lantern light when Emma arrived, evergreen garlands draped across every beam and window filling the air with the sharp scent of pine. She'd spent the morning hanging decorations with Deborah Peachey, whose constant chatter about Noah had made Emma's nerves fray like old thread pulled too tight.

"I heard he's been helping his father with the farm," Deborah said, securing a garland with practiced efficiency. "And that he went to visit Eli Fisher's shop. Do you think he'll come tonight? Everyone's wondering. Sarah said Bishop Lapp and Weaver are worried Noah might cause problems."

Sarah Mathews, Bishop Lapp's daughter, would indeed have firsthand knowledge. Now the community midwife, she had married an *Englischer doktor*—a good woman who had chosen an unconventional path while staying true to her faith. A reminder that even in Miracle Creek, not everything was as rigid as it first seemed.

Emma had made noncommittal sounds while Deborah chattered, focusing on the work, trying not to think about the possibility of seeing Noah again in a social setting, surrounded by the entire community's watchful eyes.

Now, standing in the decorated hall with the first guests arriving, Emma smoothed her dress—soft blue, like summer skies—and tried to calm her racing heart. She'd told herself the color choice meant nothing, that she'd simply grabbed the first clean dress she found. But standing here, she admitted the truth: she'd chosen this dress because Noah had once said it reminded him of forget-me-nots, the delicate flowers that grew wild near the creek where they used to meet.

Foolish. Dangerous. A betrayal of the practical path she'd chosen.

"Emma!" Deborah hurried over, her blue eyes sparkling with excitement. Miracle Creek's new schoolteacher, Deborah's vibrant red hair caught the lamplight beneath her *kapp*, as she nudged Emma to look up toward the entrance. "He's here. Noah just arrived—with his parents."

Emma's breath caught. She turned slowly toward the entrance, and there he was—Noah, standing near the doorway with Gideon and Miriam flanking him like guards. He'd dressed carefully, she noticed—his best suspenders, his shirt pressed and clean, his hair neatly combed. He was trying, making an effort to fit in, to belong again.

Their eyes met across the room. The world narrowed to that look—everything they'd been, everything they'd lost, everything that might still be possible, compressed into a heartbeat that seemed to last forever. Emma felt the pull between them like a physical thing, a cord stretched taut that wanted to snap them together.

Then Isaiah was at her elbow, his hand proprietary on her arm, his presence an anchor pulling her back to reality.

"Emma! You look lovely tonight." Isaiah's smile was warm, genuine. He was a kind man, she reminded herself. A *gut* man who deserved her full attention, not these divided loyalties and confused feelings. "I saved you a seat with my family."

"That's thoughtful, thank you." Emma let him guide her toward the Weaver section, aware that everyone was watching this small tableau—Noah's return, Isaiah's claim, Emma's choice. The community loved nothing more than a good drama, and she was apparently providing tonight's prime entertainment.

They took their seats for the singing, families gathering in their traditional arrangements. Emma found herself across from Noah, their positions in the circle putting them in direct line of sight. She tried to focus on the hymnal in her lap, on the familiar German words of the Christmas songs they'd been singing since childhood.

But when the singing began and Noah's voice joined the harmony, Emma's careful focus shattered. His rich baritone found her soprano line and wrapped around it, their voices blending as naturally as breathing. When she faltered on a verse—her voice catching on words about homecoming and belonging—Noah's voice steadied her, supported her, carried her through the difficult passage.

It was like being seventeen again, their voices rising together in the old songs, the harmony between them so natural it seemed ordained. The years fell away. They could have been teenagers stealing glances across the singing circle, the whole world contained in the space between them, everything simple and possible.

Emma's eyes filled with tears she couldn't shed, not here, not in front of everyone.

Isaiah sat beside her, singing dutifully but without particular passion, unaware of the connection flowing between her and Noah like an electrical current neither could control.

The final notes of the hymn faded into silence. The room erupted in cheerful chatter as people stood and moved toward the refreshment tables. Isaiah touched Emma's arm, saying something about getting her cider, but she barely heard him. Noah was moving through the crowd toward her, his expression intent, determined.

"Emma." His voice when he reached her was low, meant only for her ears despite the curious looks from surrounding community members. "Could we talk? Just for a moment?"

"I don't think that's a *gut* idea," she said, even as everything in her wanted to say yes, wanted to flee this crowded room and find somewhere private where they could actually speak honestly for the first time in five years.

"Please. I just—" Noah glanced around at the watching faces and lowered his voice further. "I'd love to see your bakery sometime. Hear about all your new recipes. Your father mentioned you've been expanding."

Emma's heart leaped traitorously. "Tomorrow afternoon? I'll be working late to prepare for the market. Joanna will be out on deliveries. We could talk then." The words escaped before wisdom could stop them.

"Tomorrow afternoon," Noah confirmed, relief evident in his expression.

"Noah!" Isaiah's voice cut through their conversation, too loud, too sharp. The bishop's son pushed through the crowd with barely concealed annoyance. "Don't forget about the Christmas council meeting tomorrow. Everyone's expected. We're planning the market layout."

The spell broke. Emma saw calculation in Isaiah's eyes, the deliberate interruption designed to separate her from Noah, to remind the community of Isaiah's rightful place and Noah's questionable status.

"Of course," Noah said, his jaw tightening slightly. "I'll be there."

"Gut." Isaiah's hand found Emma's elbow again, his touch firm, possessive. "Emma, your father's looking for you. Something about the bakery booth assignments."

She allowed herself to be led away, but looked back once. Noah stood alone in the crowd, watching her go, his expression a mixture of longing and resignation that made her chest ache.

The rest of the evening passed in a blur. Emma smiled and chatted and pretended everything was normal, that her world hadn't just tilted dangerously off-axis. Isaiah stayed close, attentive and proper, doing everything right while somehow making Emma feel increasingly trapped.

"You sang beautifully tonight," he said during a quiet moment, offering her a cup of cider. "Your voice has such purity. It's a gift from *Gott.*"

"Thank you." Emma sipped the cider, which tasted like ashes in her mouth. "But it is the Lord who gives His gifts as He pleases. I am but his instrument."

"I was thinking," Isaiah continued, his tone casual but his eyes intent, "perhaps after Christmas, we could make our understanding official. Announce our courtship publicly. My father thinks it would be appropriate, and your father seems agreeable. *Datt* also says it would be a *gut* match to strengthen bonds between our two communities. I know Hope Valley is not even three miles away but—"

Emma nearly choked on her cider. "Isaiah, I—I need more time to think about that."

His expression tightened almost imperceptibly. "Of course. But don't take too long, Emma. People are talking, and it wouldn't be *gut* for either of our reputations if you seem uncertain."

The implied threat was gentle but unmistakable: decide soon, or face the community's judgment for leading him on.

"I understand," Emma said, though she understood far too much—that she was being maneuvered into a corner, that her choices were narrowing by the day, that soon she'd have no choice at all.

Later, as families began departing into the cold night, Deborah grabbed Emma's arm, pulling her aside.

"Did you see the way he looked at you?" Deborah's eyes gleamed with vicarious excitement. "Noah, I mean. Like you were the only person in the room. Like nothing else existed."

"Deborah—"

"Don't 'Deborah' me. Everyone saw it. Isaiah saw it too—why do you think he was hovering over you all night like a jealous hawk?" Deborah squeezed her friend's hand. "You have to make a choice, Emma. You can't keep both of them hanging on."

"I'm not trying to keep anyone hanging on. I didn't ask for any of this."

"No, but here it is anyway." Deborah's expression softened, her usual sparkle giving way to genuine concern. "I just want you to be happy. Truly happy—not just content or dutiful. Life's too short for mere contentment."

Though the same age as Emma, Deborah often carried a wisdom beyond her years.

Emma pulled her cloak tight and stepped into the winter night, Deborah's words echoing in her mind. The snow crunched under her boots as she walked toward home, Isaiah's offer of a buggy ride politely declined. She needed space, needed air, needed to think without anyone watching or judging or expecting.

The night was clear and cold, stars brilliant against the black sky. Emma paused at the edge of town, looking back at the community hall's warm glow, then forward toward the dark path home. A crossroads, literal and metaphorical.

Behind her lay the Christmas singing, Isaiah's expectations, the community's approval, a safe and predictable future stretching out like the familiar road she'd always known.

Ahead lay uncertainty, risk, the possibility of heartbreak if she trusted Noah and he left again. But also the possibility of something real, something passionate, something that made her feel alive rather than simply dutiful. Something more than mere contentment.

Emma stood at that crossroads for a long time, the cold seeping through her cloak, before finally turning toward home. But she didn't sleep that night, staring at the ceiling instead, counting the hours until tomorrow afternoon when she'd see Noah again.

One way or another, she'd have to choose.

Chapter 5
Memories in Flour and Sugar

Emma arrived at the bakery before dawn the next morning, lighting the ovens and measuring ingredients with practiced precision while her thoughts raced ahead to the afternoon, to Noah's promised visit. The familiar work usually grounded her, but today her hands shook slightly as she measured flour, and she had to restart her count of cinnamon sticks twice.

Sleep had been impossible after the singing. She'd lain awake replaying every moment—Noah's voice blending with hers, the look in his eyes, Isaiah's possessive touch on her arm. Round and round her thoughts had spun until dawn came as a relief, giving her an excuse to flee her bed and lose herself in work.

The morning passed in a haze of customers and baking. Joanna arrived at seven, full of energy and gossip about the singing, but Emma deflected her questions with tasks—knead this dough, frost those cookies, help Mrs. Yoder choose bread for her grandchildren's visit. By noon, Joanna had given up trying to extract information and settled into her own chatter, filling the bakery with bright noise that required no response.

The afternoon lull arrived. Joanna left to deliver special orders around town, and Emma found herself alone in the bakery, jumping at every sound, heart racing each time the door bell jingled.

Three o'clock came. Then three-thirty. Emma busied

herself with tomorrow's preparations, telling herself she was foolish to have expected him, that he'd probably changed his mind, that this was for the best anyway.

The door creaked open at four.

Emma looked up from the dough she was kneading, flour dusting her hands and apron. Noah stood in the doorway, afternoon light haloing him, hesitation written across his face.

"Afternoon, sorry I'm late. The council meeting ran long."

"It's fine." Emma wiped her hands on her apron, suddenly self-conscious about the flour in her hair, the plain work dress, the mundane setting. "I'm just preparing for tomorrow's market."

Noah stepped inside, and the bakery suddenly felt smaller, the air thicker with his presence. He moved slowly, taking in the space—the worn wooden counters, the display cases filled with the day's remaining goods, the ovens radiating warmth against the winter cold.

"You've made it beautiful," he said. "The bakery. It feels like you—warm and welcoming and full of *gut* things."

Emma's cheeks heated at the compliment. She focused on the dough, kneading it with more force than necessary. "It's just a bakery."

"It's more than that. It's a home." Noah moved closer, his eyes traveling over the shelves of ingredients, the carefully organized workspace. "You always added extra ginger to the *lebkuchen*. When we were kids."

A surprised laugh escaped her despite her nervousness. "I did. I thought it made them special. My *mammi* said I was tampering with perfection, but she let me do it anyway." The memory was sweet and painful at once—

long afternoons in this very kitchen, her grandmother's patient instruction, the freedom to experiment within the bounds of tradition.

"They were special. Everything you made was special." He picked up a rolling pin, turning it in his hands, and Emma watched his fingers—stronger now, marked by calluses from hard labor, no longer the smooth hands of the boy she'd known. "Do you remember sledding on Primrose Hill? You beat me every single time."

"Because you fell off before the finish line!" The memory warmed her, thawing the careful distance she'd tried to maintain. "And then we built that enormous snowman behind the schoolhouse. You insisted on using your father's *gut* hat for it even though you knew your mother would be angry."

"She made me wear Bethany's bonnet for a week as punishment," Noah laughed, the sound rich and genuine, filling the bakery with warmth that had nothing to do with the ovens. "Worth it though. That snowman was legendary. Lasted until March."

They fell into easier conversation, past and present blending as seamlessly as ingredients in her mixing bowl. Noah's hands helped instinctively—passing the cinnamon when she reached for it, steadying the mixing bowl when it tilted, retrieving flour from the high shelf she couldn't quite reach. Each small touch sent sparks through her, electricity that made her hyperaware of every breath, every movement, every place their bodies came close to touching.

"The *Englisch* world taught me some things," Noah said, watching her roll out dough with practiced efficiency. "But nothing there smelled as *gut* as this. Nothing felt as right."

Emma's hands stilled, the rolling pin frozen mid-stroke. The words hung between them, weighted with meaning that went beyond mere reminiscence.

"Why did you leave without saying goodbye?"

The question escaped before she could stop it, raw and aching despite her efforts to sound casual. She'd meant to keep things light, pleasant, safe. Instead, five years of hurt spilled out in a single sentence that made her feel stripped bare and vulnerable.

Noah's hands stilled on the mixing bowl he'd been steadying. His jaw tightened, and for a long moment he didn't speak. Emma watched emotions flicker across his face—shame, regret, pain, something else she couldn't quite identify.

"I couldn't bear to see disappointment in your eyes," he said finally, his voice rough with emotion. "Your *datt* had made it clear I wasn't good enough for you. My *datt* thought I was throwing my life away, questioning my faith, becoming a problem. I thought..." He drew a shaky breath. "I thought leaving quietly would hurt less. For both of us. I thought if I stayed, I'd disappoint everyone eventually anyway, so why drag it out?"

"You thought I'd be disappointed?" Hurt sharpened Emma's voice to a blade, five years of suppressed anger suddenly breaking free. "You just left, Noah. No explanation. No letter. Nothing. I waited for months thinking something terrible had happened to you. That you were hurt or dead or..." Her voice broke. "Do you have any idea what that did to me? What it did to my family?"

"I know." The words came out broken. "I thought about you every single day. I tried to write letters—must have started a hundred of them. But what could I say?

That I was failing in the *Englisch* world too? That I didn't fit there either? That I was more lost out there than I'd ever been here?" He ran his hands through his hair, frustration and self-recrimination evident in every line of his body.

The air thickened between them, heavy with years of unspoken feelings and accumulated pain. Emma's eyes stung with tears she refused to shed, her throat tight with emotions she didn't know how to process. Part of her wanted to rage at him, to make him feel even a fraction of the hurt she'd carried. But another part—the part that remembered who he'd been, who they'd been together—understood that he'd been suffering too.

"I needed you," she whispered. "And you weren't there."

"I know. I'm so sorry. If I could go back—"

The door banged open. Michael strode in, his face hardening when he saw Noah standing close to his daughter, flour on both their hands, the intimacy of the scene unmistakable even if they weren't actually touching.

"What's he doing here?" Michael's voice was steel, cold and unforgiving.

"He's just—" Emma started, but her father cut her off.

"Just here to stir things up again?" Michael's eyes blazed with protective anger. "To disrupt Emma's life after she's finally found some stability? He'll leave, Emma. People like him always do. They get restless, get bored, decide the grass is greener somewhere else, and off they go without a thought for the people they hurt."

Noah stepped back, his shoulders tightening defensively. "I should go."

"Wait!" Emma reached out instinctively, but Noah was already moving toward the door, the moment shattering like the glass jars she'd dropped at the general store.

"Guard your heart, *mei dochder,*" Michael said after Noah left, his tone softening slightly as he saw the distress on his daughter's face. "Your reputation matters in this community. People are already talking about you and Noah, about Isaiah and what this means for his family. The bishop and elders are concerned. *Mamm* is concerned. We all just want what's best for you."

"And you think you know what's best for me?" Emma's voice was sharper than she'd intended, anger finally finding an outlet. "You and the bishop, all deciding my future without asking what I want?"

"We're trying to protect you from making a terrible mistake." Michael's expression was genuinely concerned, his worry for her evident despite his harsh words about Noah. "Isaiah is offering you security, respectability, a *gut* future. What is Noah offering? Five years of silence followed by pretty words and no promises?"

Emma wanted to argue, to defend Noah, to assert her right to make her own choices. But the words stuck in her throat because her *datt* wasn't entirely wrong. Noah had made no promises, no declarations of intent. He'd apologized for leaving but hadn't said he was staying. The difference mattered.

"I need to finish preparing for tomorrow," she said instead, turning back to her work, dismissing her father without directly defying him.

Michael hesitated, clearly wanting to say more, but finally left with a warning look that said this conversation wasn't over.

Alone again, Emma moved mechanically through her tasks, but her hands shook and her eyes blurred with tears. When she turned to clean up, something caught her eye—a small wooden star on the counter where Noah had been standing, carved with delicate precision.

She picked it up with flour-covered fingers, recognizing it immediately. The same design Noah had given her that last Christmas before he left, the one she'd treasured until she'd finally forced herself to pack it away with other painful reminders of their relationship.

He'd kept the design all these years. Remembered it. Carved her a new one.

Emma traced the familiar pattern, feeling the smooth wood worn by his hands, seeing the care in every line and curve. This wasn't just a carving—it was a message, a reminder, a promise of something, though she didn't know what.

She tucked it into her apron pocket and returned to work, but the star's presence against her hip felt like a secret, a connection she couldn't quite sever no matter how hard wisdom tried to convince her otherwise.

That evening, after closing the bakery, Emma walked home slowly through the winter dusk. The town looked peaceful in the fading light, smoke curling from chimneys, lanterns beginning to glow in windows. Her life here was good—safe, comfortable, predictable. Marrying Isaiah would cement that security, would please her father and the community, would fulfill all the expectations she'd been raised to meet.

But it wouldn't make her happy. Not truly, deeply, soul-singing happy the way she'd been during those brief moments with Noah before her father interrupted.

The realization felt like betrayal—of Isaiah, of her father, of the community that had raised and nurtured her. But it also felt like truth, undeniable and stark.

Emma stood outside her house, looking at the warm

light spilling from the windows, knowing her family waited inside with dinner and conversation and the comfortable routines of home. She could go inside, could slip back into the role of dutiful daughter, could move forward with the plan everyone had laid out for her.

Or she could choose differently. Choose risk and uncertainty and the possibility of heartbreak. Choose the chance, however slim, of something real.

The wooden star pressed against her hip through her apron pocket, a constant reminder of choices not yet made.

Emma took a deep breath and went inside.

Chapter 6
The Bishop's Warning

Sunday service felt different with Noah back in the community. Emma was hyperaware of him sitting with his family across the room, of the way people's eyes flickered between them during hymns, of the whispers that followed like shadows whenever they were in the same space.

Bishop Lapp rose to address the congregation, his weathered face grave in the morning light filtering through the windows. The sermon's subject became clear quickly: steadfastness, resisting worldly temptations, remaining faithful to community traditions and the path Gott had laid out for each of them.

And the bishop's eyes kept landing on Noah.

"Each of us carries stories of struggle and redemption," Bishop Lapp intoned, his voice carrying easily through the hushed room. "Tonight we're reminded that forgiveness and community are our strength. But we must also remember that actions have consequences. When we stray from the path, when we pursue our own desires above *Gott's* will and community welfare, we risk not only our own souls but the souls of those around us."

Emma felt her cheeks burn. The message wasn't subtle. The entire community understood who the bishop was talking about, who the cautionary tale was aimed at. She kept her eyes fixed on her lap, refusing to look up, refusing to see the judgment in people's faces.

"Some among us have returned after time in the world," the bishop continued. "We welcome them with open hearts, as the father welcomed the prodigal son. But welcome requires transformation. It requires proof of changed hearts and renewed commitment. We cannot allow the poison of worldliness to seep into our community, corrupting our young people, leading them astray with false promises of excitement and freedom beyond our borders."

The words hung in the air like a sentencing. Emma risked a glance toward Noah and immediately wished she hadn't. His face was carefully blank, but she could see the tightness around his eyes, the way his jaw clenched with suppressed emotion. He was being publicly castigated, warned, put on notice that his presence was tolerated but not yet trusted.

After the service, Emma watched the bishop call Noah aside, gesturing toward his office with a movement that brooked no refusal. Her stomach knotted with anxiety as they disappeared through the door, the entire congregation pretending not to watch while watching avidly.

Inside the bishop's office, the walls felt close, confining. Noah stood straight, hands clasped in front of him, while Bishop Lapp settled into his chair behind the worn wooden desk that had served the community's spiritual leader for thirty years.

"Sit," the bishop commanded, his voice gentler than it had been during the sermon but still carrying unmistakable authority.

Noah sat, feeling like a child called to account for misbehavior.

"Your return has caused quite a stir," Bishop Lapp began, his fingers steepled in front of him. "People have concerns. Valid concerns, I should add."

"I came back to be with my family, to be part of the community again," Noah said, keeping his voice respectful despite the defensiveness rising in his chest.

"But your intentions bear scrutiny." The bishop's eyes were sharp as flint, missing nothing. "You left once, abandoning your responsibilities, your family, your commitments. What assurance do we have that you won't do so again? What proof can you offer that you've truly returned, not just in body but in spirit?"

Noah had no good answer. What proof could he offer beyond his word, which had already been broken once? "I understand your concerns, Sir. All I can say is that I'm here, I'm willing to work, to contribute, to earn back the trust I lost."

"Words are easy, Noah. Actions matter more." The bishop leaned forward, stroked his gray beard. "Your name has resurfaced regarding Emma Mast—particularly in relation to Isaiah's intentions toward her."

Noah's stomach dropped. Of course this would come up. Of course his presence would be seen as interference in Isaiah's careful courtship.

"I haven't—I'm not trying to interfere with anything," Noah said, though even to his own ears the protest sounded weak.

"Intentions matter less than perceptions in this case. Isaiah has formally requested permission to court Emma. He spoke with her father yesterday, with my full blessing and encouragement. He would be an excellent match for her—stable, devout, committed to our ways. Everything a woman like Emma needs."

The unspoken comparison hung heavy: *Everything you're not.*

"I understand," Noah said, though understanding and accepting were different things entirely.

"Do you?" The bishop's gaze intensified. "Because your presence is complicating matters. Emma is a *gut* woman, but she's also young and perhaps more susceptible to romantic notions than is wise. Your return, your history with her—it's creating confusion, making it difficult for her to see clearly what path she should take."

"Are you asking me to stay away from her?" Noah asked cautiously.

"I'm suggesting that you be mindful of the consequences of your actions. Emma deserves stability, not uncertainty. She deserves a man who will stay, not one who might disappear at the first sign of difficulty." The bishop's tone softened slightly. "However, I also recognize that you may wish to prove yourself, to show this community that you've changed—if you indeed have changed."

Noah sensed the subtle opening. "I do want to prove myself, Sir."

"Then I have a proposal." The bishop pulled out a sheet of paper covered in neat, precise handwriting. "Widow Kauffman needs help. Her roof is failing, and she requires an additional room for the winter months. I would like you to lead the construction project. Organize the men, manage the work, see it through to completion. It would demonstrate your dedication, your commitment to the welfare of the community."

It was a test—a very public one. Every action, every decision would be observed, judged. But it was also an opportunity to show he had changed, to prove he possessed leadership and steadfastness.

"I'll do it," Noah said without hesitation.

"Gut." The bishop made a note on his paper, then added almost casually, "You might also reconnect with Emma through the work—she often brings food to work crews."

Noah frowned. What was the shrewd old bishop up to? Was he trying to smooth the course of true love—and if so, for whom?

The bishop's tone grew firm again. "But understand this: if you wish to fully rejoin us, to be baptized and accepted as a full member of this community again, you must complete baptism preparations. The classes begin after Christmas and continue for six months. During that time, you must demonstrate absolute commitment. That means..." He paused significantly. "That means refraining from private meetings with Emma until your intentions and commitments are clear. The community must have certainty about your path before you can court anyone, particularly someone as valued as Emma Mast."

Noah's hands clenched on the arms of his chair. Six months of staying away from Emma while Isaiah had free rein to court her, to win her over, to convince her to accept his proposal. Six months of proving himself while his heart remained in limbo.

"I understand," he said, though the words tasted like ash in his mouth.

"I hope you do. Because if you fail—if you leave again, if you disrupt Isaiah's courtship without offering Emma any real alternative, if you prove unreliable—there will be consequences. Not just for you, but for your entire family. Your father has worked hard to maintain his standing in this community despite your absence. Don't make him pay for your choices again."

The threat was subtle but unmistakable. Behave, or your family suffers.

"When do I start with Widow Kauffman's house?" Noah asked, changing the subject because he didn't trust himself to respond to the threat without anger seeping into his voice.

"Tomorrow. I'll announce it at this evening's meeting." The bishop stood, signaling the conversation's end. "Don't disappoint us, Noah. This community has a long memory for both loyalty and betrayal." He paused, letting the weight of his words settle. "And also of forgiveness. But before forgiveness comes, there must be true repentance."

Noah left the office feeling like he'd been stripped bare and rebuilt wrong, like all his pieces had been rearranged into a shape that didn't quite fit. The congregation had dispersed for the midday meal, families heading home or gathering in small groups to share food and fellowship.

Noah found Eli standing by his buggy, waiting for Lorraine Andrews—the girl he was courting. Lorraine, one of postman Joseph Andrews' three daughters, was still deep in conversation with Anna Hostetler and Sarah Mathews. Concern for his friend showed clearly in Eli's expression.

"So… how bad was it?" Eli asked, his tone a mixture of curiosity and worry.

"I'm leading the construction project for Widow Kauffman. And I have to stay away from Emma until I complete baptism preparations."

Eli winced. "Six months of classes. That's a long time."

"Long enough for Isaiah to convince her to marry him." Noah couldn't keep the bitterness from his voice.

"Maybe. Or maybe if it's meant to be, six months won't matter." Eli clapped his friend on the shoulder. "Focus on the work. Do it well. Show them who you are now, not who you were when you left."

Sound advice, but it didn't ease the knot in Noah's chest or the fear that he'd come home only to lose Emma all over again, this time to a better man who'd never left in the first place.

That evening, as twilight painted the sky in shades of purple and gold, Noah walked to the council meeting at the community hall. The building was already full, families gathered to discuss the Christmas market, charity projects, and other community business.

Emma was there with her father, sitting toward the front. She didn't look at Noah as he entered, but he saw her shoulders tense, saw her fingers tighten on the notebook in her lap. Isaiah sat beside her, attentive and proper, his presence a declaration of intent that everyone recognized.

Noah took a seat toward the back, trying to be unobtrusive, but he felt the weight of curious and skeptical gazes. The prodigal returned, on trial before the community he'd abandoned.

Bishop Lapp called the meeting to order and quickly moved through routine business before arriving at what everyone was really waiting to hear.

"As many of you know, Widow Kauffman is in need of assistance. Her roof requires repair, and we've decided to add a small room to help her through the winter. This will be a community project, with all able-bodied men contributing time and labor." The bishop paused, his gaze finding Noah. "I've asked Noah Albrecht to lead this project. He has experience with construction from his time away, and this will be an opportunity for him to demonstrate his commitment to our community's welfare."

Murmurs rippled through the room—some approving, some skeptical. Noah felt his face flush but kept his expression neutral. This was his test, his chance to prove himself, and he couldn't afford to show weakness or doubt.

"Work begins tomorrow at dawn," the bishop continued. "Noah will organize the labor and materials. We expect the project to be completed before the first major snowstorm."

More discussion followed about other matters, but Noah barely heard it. He was too aware of Emma sitting across the room, too conscious of the responsibility he'd just been given, too anxious about the next few months and what they would mean for his future.

After the meeting adjourned, families lingered to socialize and make plans. Noah tried to slip out unnoticed, but Gideon caught his arm.

"Don't embarrass me," his father said quietly. "Do this right."

"I will."

"And stay away from Emma. I heard about your visit to the bakery." Gideon's expression was stern. "Isaiah is a *gut* match for her. Don't ruin it with your presence."

Noah nodded, unable to speak past the lump in his throat. Even his own father thought he was more liability than asset, more problem than solution.

Outside, the winter air bit at his exposed skin, but Noah welcomed the cold. It was honest, straightforward, unlike the complicated web of expectations and judgments he'd walked into by coming home.

He started walking, not ready to return to the farm, needing movement and space to process everything. His feet carried him without conscious direction until he found himself at the frozen pond where he and Emma used to meet.

The ice gleamed under the rising moon, smooth and perfect, unmarked by skate blades this early in the season. Noah stood at the edge, remembering summer afternoons that had stretched into autumn evenings and winter nights. Emma's hand in his. Her laughter echoing across the ice. The promises they'd whispered, believing they'd last forever.

All of it gone now. All of it impossible to reclaim.

He knelt at the pond's edge, despite the cold, the frozen ground hard beneath his knees, and tried to pray. Tried to find some guidance, some assurance that he was on the right path, that coming home hadn't been a terrible mistake.

But the words wouldn't come.

"You look troubled."

Noah turned. Widow Kauffman stood on the path behind him, her shawl wrapped tight against the cold, her weathered face kind in the moonlight.

"Just thinking," Noah said, standing and brushing snow from his knees.

"About Emma?" The widow's directness was surprising but not unwelcome. She, like everyone else in Miracle Creek, had seen the teen romance unfold.

"Among other things."

"May I tell you something?" Without waiting for permission, she settled onto a fallen log nearby, patting the space beside her in invitation.

Noah sat, grateful for company even if he didn't particularly want conversation.

"When I was young, I loved a man who felt called to leave our community," the widow began, her eyes distant, lost in memory. "We shared moments that stitched our souls together. But when he left, I didn't tell him how I felt. I stayed true to my faith, but I regretted my silence."

Her eyes shimmered with the ghost of lost possibilities, and for the first time, Noah glimpsed the depths of her own heartache.

"You have no regrets for remaining?" he asked, his voice edged with genuine curiosity.

"I do not regret staying true to my faith," she said, her tone steadfast yet tender, "but I regret not speaking my heart before he departed. Perhaps he may have returned. Perhaps we could have found a different road. I married Amos Kauffman a year later, but I always wondered what might have been with the other man." She paused, her gaze faraway. "Marriages—even those of convenience or obligation—can be happy. Love can grow from small seeds. But true love… true love is magical. It's a once—or maybe twice—in-a-lifetime kind of thing. Sometimes, the courage to voice what we feel can be the most difficult journey of all."

The words settled over him like a delicate snowfall, softening the rigid edges of his apprehension.

"I've been afraid," Noah admitted, "afraid of losing everything if I embrace what's in my heart."

"True faith means trusting Gott with your future," she replied, leaning closer, her warmth filling the air. "Trust that what is meant for you will not be lost by your own honesty."

"Sometimes the bravest thing is to speak honestly, even when the outcome is uncertain," the widow continued. "The bishop and the elders—they mean well. They want to protect the community, maintain our ways. But they are not infallible. They don't know every heart. They can't predict every future."

"Are you saying I should disobey the bishop?"

"I'm saying you should be honest about what you want and what you're willing to do to get it. Make your choices deliberately, not by default or fear." She straightened, preparing to leave. "The roof project—it's a test, yes. But it's also an opportunity. Use it wisely."

She walked away, leaving Noah alone with his thoughts and the frozen pond and the weight of decisions that felt too large for one person to carry.

He pulled out the chess piece—the king—from his pocket, studying it in the moonlight. For months, he'd carried it as a reminder of what he'd lost. Now it felt like a challenge: what was he willing to do to reclaim what mattered? What risks would he take? What sacrifices would he make?

Noah stood, pocketing the piece, and started toward home. Tomorrow the real work began—building Widow Kauffman's room, proving himself to the community, finding a way to show Emma he'd changed without violating the bishop's edict.

Six months felt like an eternity. But maybe, if he was patient and careful and lucky, it would be enough.

Chapter 7
The Widow's Roof

Dawn broke cold and clear over Widow Kauffman's property. Noah stood before the gathered men—Eli, Michael, Gideon, and a dozen others—clipboard in hand, trying to project more confidence than he felt. The weight of community scrutiny pressed down like the heavy tool belt around his waist.

"Thank you all for coming," he said, his breath fogging in the frigid air. His voice came out steady, which was a relief. "Together we'll make sure Widow Kauffman's home stands strong through winter."

He'd spent half the night planning, sketching rough designs, making lists of materials and tasks. Now he consulted those notes, assigning work according to each man's strengths—something he'd learned in the English construction world but tempered with knowledge of Amish methods and community dynamics.

"Eli, I want you on the foundation work. Your carpentry skills will be essential for the support beams." Noah moved down his list to Melvin Zook. "Melvin, you'll lead the framing crew. Use the lumber we've already cut, but check each piece for soundness. We can't afford weak joints."

He continued through the assignments, pleased to see men nodding and moving to their tasks with minimal resistance. Some skepticism remained in their eyes, but they were willing to follow his lead, at least for now.

Gideon watched from the sidelines, his expression unreadable. Noah had asked him to oversee materials and supplies, a position of responsibility that acknowledged his father's experience while not putting him in direct conflict with Noah's leadership. The dynamic was awkward, but it seemed to be working.

As morning progressed, the rhythm of construction took over—hammers ringing, saws cutting, men calling out measurements and instructions. Noah moved between stations, checking work, answering questions, solving problems as they arose. The *Englisch* techniques he'd learned blended surprisingly well with traditional Amish methods, creating something stronger than either alone.

"This joint here," Eli called out, gesturing to a beam connection. "You're using a different technique than I'm familiar with."

Noah explained the mortise-and-tenon variation he'd learned in Columbus, showing how it provided extra stability while still using traditional hand tools. Eli nodded slowly, then smiled.

"That's clever. Stronger than our usual method but still honors the old ways." He clapped Noah on the shoulder. "You've learned some *gut* things out there."

The praise warmed Noah more than he wanted to admit. Around him, he felt the subtle shift in attitude—men starting to see him as competent rather than merely tolerated, as someone who'd gained valuable knowledge rather than simply abandoned his roots.

By midday, they'd made remarkable progress. The foundation was solid, framing was beginning to take shape, and the roof supports were being prepared. Noah allowed himself a moment of satisfaction, surveying the work with a craftsman's eye.

Then Emma arrived.

She came with Deborah and Joanna, all three carrying baskets heavy with food. The delicious smells of fresh bread and hearty stew cut through the scents of sawdust and sweat, and the men's energy visibly lifted at the promise of a hearty meal.

"Thank you for bringing lunch," Noah said formally, painfully aware of how many eyes were watching this interaction. He kept his distance, maintained professional courtesy, gave no one reason to comment on impropriety. But his heart raced, and he couldn't help noticing how the winter sun caught the blonde wisps of hair escaping her *kapp*, how her cheeks pinked from the cold made her blue eyes seem brighter.

"You've made *gut* progress," Emma observed, surveying the construction with what seemed like genuine interest. "Widow Kauffman will be so pleased."

"It's a community effort." Noah gestured to the working men. "Everyone's contributed."

"But you're leading it." Her eyes met his briefly. "That takes skill."

The moment stretched, loaded with everything they couldn't say, before Joanna called Emma over to help serve food. Noah forced himself to turn away, to focus on his crew, to not watch Emma move among the men with grace and kindness that made his chest ache.

Michael appeared at his elbow, his expression carefully neutral. "The framing is solid. You've done well with the design."

Coming from Emma's father, this was high praise indeed. "*Denki.* I couldn't have done it without everyone's help."

"Don't let it go to your head." But Michael's tone lacked real bite. "There's still plenty of work ahead, and winter weather can turn vicious without warning."

As if summoned by the mention, dark clouds began gathering on the horizon. The men noticed too, glancing skyward with the practiced concern of people whose livelihoods depended on weather.

"Storm coming," town blacksmith John Hostetler said unnecessarily, joining Noah and Michael. "We should secure everything."

Noah assessed the situation quickly. They'd made excellent progress, but a sudden storm could undo hours of work if materials weren't properly protected. "Everyone! We need to cover the lumber and secure any loose materials. Move fast!"

The men sprang into action with the coordinated efficiency of people used to working together. Noah directed the effort, pulling together a plan on the fly—tarps here, weights there, vulnerable sections reinforced or temporarily dismantled.

The wind picked up, bitter and sharp. Snow began falling in thick flakes that quickly obscured visibility. What had been a clear day turned dark and threatening within minutes.

"The framework!" John shouted over the rising wind. "If we lose it, we'll have to start over!"

Noah's mind raced. The English construction sites had taught him about emergency measures, temporary supports, ways to protect work-in-progress from the elements. "We need to build a shelter over it! Quick temporary structure, just enough to break the wind and keep the worst of the snow off!"

Some of the men looked skeptical—they'd never done

such a thing—but Gideon nodded sharply. "Do it. Noah, tell us what you need."

Working against the clock and the storm, Noah directed the construction of a makeshift shelter using spare lumber and every tarp they could find. The men worked with impressive speed, trusting Noah's design even when it differed from their usual methods.

Emma and the other women had taken shelter in Widow Kauffman's house, but Noah was aware of faces at the windows, watching. More witnesses to his success or failure.

The shelter came together with minutes to spare before the full force of the storm hit. As the men huddled beneath their improvised protection, catching their breath and checking that everything was secure, Noah felt a shift in the group's dynamic. They'd worked together to solve a problem, and his leadership had been crucial to that success.

"Well done," Gideon said quietly, just for Noah's ears. "That was smart thinking."

The simple praise from his *datt* meant more than Noah could express. He nodded, throat tight, and focused on ensuring everyone was accounted for and safe.

They waited out the worst of the storm under the shelter, men sharing body warmth and quiet conversation. When it finally passed, leaving the landscape blanketed in fresh snow, they emerged to find their work protected, nothing lost except time.

"Tomorrow we'll make up what we lost today," Eli said, his confidence in the project—and in Noah— evident. "We've got a *gut* design and a *gut* crew."

As the men departed, Noah stayed behind to do a final check of the site. Emma emerged from the widow's house, her shawl wrapped tight, carrying a small basket.

"I saved you some food," she said, approaching carefully, aware they were technically alone even though the widow and her schwester and friend were still inside. "You didn't eat earlier."

"Thank you." Noah took the basket, his fingers brushing hers for just a moment—a spark that shot through him like lightning despite the cold. "How is Widow Kauffman?"

"Grateful. She was watching from the window, saw how you protected the work. She wanted me to tell you that you have her appreciation and her prayers."

They stood in the snow, the world quiet around them, the intimacy of the moment both precious and dangerous. Noah wanted to say so much—about the bishop's restrictions, about his plans for baptism, about the six months stretching ahead like an eternity. But the words stuck in his throat.

"I should go," Emma said finally, though she didn't move.

"Emma—" Noah started, then stopped. What could he say that wouldn't make things worse? *"Denki.* For the food. For being here today."

She nodded, something like understanding passing between them, then hurried back toward the house. Noah watched her go, nodded to the women watching him from the window, the basket warm in his cold hands, his heart full of things he couldn't voice.

Tomorrow he'd return to this site and continue building. Tomorrow he'd keep proving himself to the community, keep working toward baptism and acceptance and the right to openly court Emma.

But tonight, he had this moment—Emma's kindness,

his father's approval, the crew's respect earned through honest work. It wasn't everything he wanted, but it was a start.

It had to be enough.

Chapter 8
Snowbound

"We should gather boughs for the market decorations," Emma said when Noah appeared at the bakery two days after the storm. She'd been expecting him, had actually been watching for him through the window, which was foolish and dangerous but undeniable.

The bishop's restrictions hung between them like a physical barrier, but the widow's construction project provided legitimate reasons for them to cross paths. Emma had reasoned that discussing community business couldn't be forbidden, even if her heart raced at the sight of him standing in her doorway, snow dusting his shoulders like stars.

"Would you help?" The question came out breathless despite her attempt at casual.

"I'd be happy to."

An hour later, they set out in Noah's sleigh, bells jingling softly as they glided over fresh, untouched snow. Away from town. Away from prying eyes. The forest bordering Hope Valley stretched before them—pristine, secluded—transforming the world into a quiet expanse of white, broken only by the rhythmic breathing of the horse and the rapid, synchronized beating of their own hearts.

This was dangerous. Emma knew it even as she settled into the seat beside Noah, accepting the blanket he offered, feeling the warmth of his body so close to hers. They were supposed to be maintaining distance, being proper, giving no one reason to gossip. But the Christmas market needed decorations, and gathering evergreen boughs was legitimate community work, and surely no one could object to two people completing a necessary task together.

Except Emma knew the task could have been done alone or with Joanna, Deborah or with any number of other people. She'd chosen Noah, and he'd accepted, and they were both pretending this was purely practical when they both knew better.

"Tell me about the *Englisch* world," she said as they drove deeper into the forest, suddenly needing to understand what had pulled him away, what he'd found out there that Miracle Creek couldn't provide. "What was it really like?"

Noah was quiet for a moment, guiding the horse, Clover, around a fallen log half-buried in snow. "Overwhelming at first. So many people, so much noise. The cities never sleep—there's always traffic, always lights, always something happening." He paused, searching for words. "I worked construction in Columbus. Big projects—office buildings, apartments, things that took months or years to complete. The scale was incredible, nothing like building a barn or a house here."

"Did you like it?"

"Sometimes. The work was interesting, challenging in different ways than here. I learned new techniques, worked with people from everywhere—Mexico, China, Somalia. Amazing how different we all were but how similar too. Everyone just wanting to make a living, feed their families, have something to show for their labor."

Emma listened, fascinated and a little frightened by the window into a world she'd never see. "What did you do when you weren't working?"

"At first? Nothing really. I was too overwhelmed, too lonely. I'd go back to my apartment—this tiny room I rented above a grocery store—and just sit there wondering what I was doing." He smiled wryly. "Took me months to start exploring, to see movies or go to restaurants or visit museums. Even then, I always felt like an outsider looking in, never quite fitting."

"Is that why you came back?"

"Part of it." Noah's hands tightened on the reins. "I thought I'd find something out there—purpose, freedom, myself. But the longer I stayed, the more lost I felt. Like I'd walked away from the only map I had and couldn't find my way without it."

They reached the section of forest where evergreens grew thick, their branches heavy with snow. Noah helped Emma down from the sleigh, his hands on her waist for just a moment longer than strictly necessary, sending warmth flooding through her despite the cold.

Clover was their only witness, watching quietly as they worked side by side—cutting boughs, loading them into the sleigh, slipping effortlessly into conversation. Each word and glance carried the ease of familiarity, reminding Emma of summers long past: lazy afternoons, whispered secrets, and the rare, unspoken certainty that they were the only two people in the world who truly understood each other.

"I want to create something at the bakery that honors tradition but isn't afraid of change," she found herself saying, articulating dreams she'd barely admitted to herself. "Something that shows respect for the past while embracing possibility. Is that prideful? Wrong? The bishop's sermon about staying true to our ways made me wonder if wanting more is sinful."

"I don't think wanting to grow and create is sinful," Noah said carefully. "Maybe it depends on the spirit behind it—are you seeking glory for yourself or trying to serve others better? Only you can answer that."

"I'm not sure I know the difference anymore." Emma secured a bundle of pine branches. "Sometimes I think I just want to prove I'm more than what everyone expects. That I have ideas and skills worth recognizing. But then I wonder if that's exactly the kind of pride the bishop warns against."

"Or maybe it's the image of *Gott* in you—the creative impulse, the desire to make something beautiful and useful. Maybe we honor *Gott* by using the gifts He gave us, not by burying them to seem humble."

The words resonated deep in Emma's chest, giving voice to feelings she'd struggled to articulate. "How did you get so wise?"

Noah laughed. "I'm not wise. I'm just someone who made a lot of mistakes and spent five years thinking about them."

They continued working, but now Emma found herself stealing glances at him—noting the way he moved with easy strength, the care he took to cut branches cleanly so the trees wouldn't be damaged, the small smile that played at his lips when he caught her looking.

Dangerous. This was so dangerous.

Snow began to fall more heavily. Clover whinnied, shifting nervously and pawing at the sodden ground. Emma lifted her eyes to the sky and realized, too late, that the clouds had thickened ominously while they worked—

too caught up in each other to notice the weather turning against them.

"We should head back," Noah said, concern creeping into his voice.

But when he tried to move the sleigh, there was a sickening crack. The runner had hit a hidden rock or log, fracturing badly enough that continuing would risk serious damage.

Noah examined it, his expression grim. "It's broken. We can't ride back on this—we'd destroy the sleigh completely and possibly hurt the horse."

Emma's heart began to race, and not from fear of the weather. They were stranded, alone, in increasingly dangerous conditions. "How far are we from town?"

"Too far to walk in this storm." Noah stood, brushing snow from his pants, his mind clearly racing through options. "There's an old hunting cabin nearby—my father used to bring us here when I was young. It should still be intact. We can shelter there until the storm passes."

They unhitched Clover, Noah taking the mare's lead rope while Emma grabbed as many supplies as she could carry from the sleigh. The walk to the cabin felt longer than it probably was, each step a struggle against wind that seemed determined to push them back, snow so thick it was hard to see more than a few feet ahead.

When the cabin finally emerged—a small, weathered structure barely visible through the curtain of white— Emma felt relief so sharp she nearly cried. Noah wrestled the door open against the accumulation of snow, ushering her inside before securing Clover in the lean-to attached to the cabin's side.

He patted the mare's nose, a gentle reassurance before

stepping toward the warmth of the cabin. Reaching into his breaches, he pulled out a peppermint. "It will be okay, old friend. Trust in *Gott*."

He leaned his face into Clover's nuzzle, inhaling the warmth and scent of the animal. The comment surprised him—he could speak of *Gott* to a horse when he could not, would not, speak to himself about Him. What did that mean? Perhaps it meant *Gott* was not as distant as he had imagined.

Inside, the cabin was simple but solid: a single room with a sturdy hearth, wooden floors worn smooth by years of use, and the faint, comforting smell of pine. It offered refuge, however modest, from the storm outside. The furniture consisted of a rough table, two chairs, and a narrow cot in the corner. Dust covered everything, but the roof appeared intact, which was all that mattered.

Noah immediately began building a fire, his movements efficient from long practice. Emma unpacked their emergency supplies—dried meat, bread, matches, a small pot for melting snow. They'd have food and warmth. They'd survive.

But they were alone together, likely for hours, possibly overnight if the storm didn't break. The impropriety of it made Emma's stomach clench with a mixture of anxiety and something else she didn't want to examine too closely.

"We'll be safe here," Noah said, as if reading her thoughts. "The storm will pass, and then we can walk— or perhaps ride—back or send someone for the sleigh. It's not ideal, but it could be worse."

Emma's heart fluttered at the thought of riding with him again: pressed close together, gripping tightly as Clover surged through the snow-covered meadows. The memory thrilled her, terrified her—made her feel young and reckless all over again.

Noah stoked the fire, and the flames licked at the kindling before reaching the larger logs. Warmth spread through the cabin, chasing back the cold that had seeped into her bones. Emma moved closer to the hearth, hands outstretched, trying not to dwell on the fact that they were trapped together, that the community's judgment would not be far from their minds, that every glance and touch could be misinterpreted.

"I'm sorry," Noah said quietly. "I should have been paying more attention to the weather. This is my fault."

"We're both responsible. I wasn't watching either." Emma turned to face him, finding him much closer than she'd realized, his face illuminated by firelight, shadows dancing across the scar on his cheek. "Noah, what happened to you? In the *Englisch* world? How did you get that scar?"

He touched his face self-consciously, as if he'd forgotten the mark was there. "Bar fight. I wasn't even part of it—just tried to help a woman who was being harassed. Got a broken bottle across the face for my trouble. Twelve stitches and a permanent reminder of how violent that world can be."

Emma winced, imagining the pain, the fear, the loneliness of recovering in a place where no one knew him, no one cared for him. "I'm sorry."

"I'm not. The scar reminds me that running away doesn't solve anything. You just trade one set of problems for another, often worse ones." He settled onto the floor near the fire, gesturing for her to take one of the chairs. "I learned a lot out there—skills, techniques, ways of seeing the world. But I also learned that home isn't a place you escape from. It's something you carry with you, and if you can't make peace with it, you'll never be at peace anywhere."

They sat in comfortable silence for a while, the only sounds the crackling fire and the howling wind outside. Emma found herself studying Noah in the flickering light —really looking at him for the first time since he'd returned. He was different now, harder in some ways but also somehow more settled, more sure of himself despite his obvious uncertainty about his place in the community.

"What do you want, Noah?" The question slipped out before she could stop it. "Really want? Not what your father wants or the bishop wants or the community expects. What do you want for your life?"

Noah remembered Widow Kaufmann's words: *"True faith means trusting Gott with your future. Trust that what is meant for you will not be lost by your own honesty."*

He took a deep breath then met her eyes across the fire. "You."

The single word hit Emma like a physical blow, stealing her breath. "Noah—"

"I'm sorry. I shouldn't have said that. The bishop made it clear I need to complete baptism preparations before I can court anyone. But you asked what I want, and that's the truth. I came back for my family, yes. To make amends, to prove I've changed. But mostly?" His voice dropped lower, rougher. "I came back for you. Everything else—the baptism, the work projects, trying to earn the community's trust—it's all means to an end. And the end is being able to stand before your father and the bishop and everyone else and say I'm worthy of you."

Emma's hands trembled as she clasped them in her lap. "What if I've changed too?" Her voice shook. "What if I'm not the girl you remember? What if five years has made us into different people who don't fit together anymore?"

"Then we'll discover that together." Noah shifted closer, still maintaining respectful distance but closing the gap between them. "But Emma, I don't think we've changed that much. Not in the ways that matter. When I saw you at the general store, when we talked in the bakery, when our voices found each other at the singing —it all felt right. Like coming home to something I'd forgotten I needed."

"The bishop said—"

"I know what the bishop said. Six months of baptism preparation. No private meetings. Prove my commitment to the community." Noah's jaw tightened. "But we're here now, through no fault of our own. The storm trapped us. And maybe... maybe that's *Gott* giving us a chance to be honest with each other before the community and the expectations and everyone else's plans get in the way."

Emma's heart hammered against her ribs. Everything she'd carefully constructed—her acceptance of Isaiah's courtship, her resignation to a practical marriage, her determination to be sensible—crumbled like dried leaves. "Isaiah has asked permission to court me formally. My *datt* approves. Bishop Lapp approves. Everyone thinks it's a *gut* match."

"Do you though?"

"He's kind. Steady. Devoted to the church and community. He'd be a *gut* husband and father. He'd never leave or break promises or make me wonder if he'd disappear one morning without explanation." The words tumbled out, defensive and hurt mixing together.

Noah flinched. "I deserved that."

"*Ja.* You did." Emma stood, needing movement, pacing the small cabin. "Do you have any idea what it was like? Waiting for word, not knowing if you were alive or dead or simply done with me? My father forbade me from speaking your name. The community whispered about how foolish I'd been to trust you. And I had to smile and pretend I was fine while everything inside me was broken."

"I know. I'm so sorry." Noah stood too, his hands clenched at his sides as if physically restraining himself from reaching for her. "I was wrong. Selfish. I convinced myself I was protecting you by leaving, but I was really just a coward running from hard conversations and harder choices. I hurt you, and I hurt my family, and I can never undo that. All I can do is try to be better now."

"How do I know you won't run again? How do I trust that when things get difficult—and they will get difficult—you won't decide it's easier to leave than to stay and work through problems?" Emma's voice broke. "I can't go through that again, Noah. I can't."

"You're right. Words aren't enough." Noah pulled something from his pocket—a carved wooden heart, no bigger than his palm, the grain of the wood silky smooth from hours of patient work. "I made this while I was away. Started it about a year after I left, finished it last month. The whole time I worked on it, I thought about you. About what I'd thrown away. About whether I'd ever have the courage to come back and face what I'd done."

He held it out to her, and Emma took it with trembling hands. The carving was exquisite—a heart with intricate details of intertwined vines and tiny flowers, forget-me-nots, she realized with a catch in her throat. The symbolism wasn't subtle.

"I'm not asking you to choose me over Isaiah right now," Noah continued, his voice steady despite the emotion in his eyes. "I'm asking you to give me six months. Let me complete the baptism preparation. Let me prove I can stay, that I can be the man you deserve. And at the end of that time, if I've proven myself, if I'm baptized and fully part of this community again... then let me court you properly. Let me show you that what we had wasn't just young foolishness but something real and lasting."

"And if I'm married to Isaiah by then?"

The question hung in the cold air. Noah's expression crumpled, but he nodded. "Then I'll accept that. I'll know I was too late, that I threw away my chance and have no one to blame but myself. But I can't not tell you how I feel because of fear." Widow Kauffman's words buoyed him. "Emma, please—don't marry him just because it's safe or expected or because you're trying to prove you've moved on from me. If you love him, truly love him, then that's different. But if you're just settling..." He took a shaky breath. "You deserve more than settling. You deserve someone who makes you feel alive."

Emma clutched the wooden heart, its weight substantial in her palm. Everything Noah said resonated with the doubts she'd been suppressing about Isaiah, about the future she'd been trying to convince herself to accept. But trust was so hard after being hurt so badly.

"I don't know if I can wait six months in limbo, not knowing which way my life will go," she admitted.

"I'm not asking you to wait in limbo. I'm asking you to live your life—work in the bakery, spend time with your family, pursue your dreams of new recipes and innovation. Just... don't close the door completely. Don't accept Isaiah's proposal without giving yourself time to be sure it's what you truly want."

The fire crackled, sending sparks up the chimney. Outside, the storm continued to rage, as if nature itself demanded they face these truths before returning to the careful pretense of their separate lives.

Emma moved closer to the fire, needing its warmth, needing time to think. Noah didn't press her, didn't demand an answer. He simply waited, patient in a way the boy she'd known had never been. Five years had changed him—not just the external scars but something deeper, some kernel of maturity earned through suffering and loneliness.

"Tell me about the *Englisch* world," she said finally, not ready to answer his implicit question but not wanting to waste this rare moment of honesty either. "Not just the construction work. Tell me about the life you lived there."

Noah settled back down by the fire, and Emma joined him, sitting close enough to share warmth but not quite touching. And in the firelight, with the storm raging outside their small shelter, Noah began to talk.

He told her about the loneliness of city living, about anonymous crowds where you could go days without anyone really seeing you. About the overwhelming choices—hundreds of kinds of bread at the grocery store, dozens of churches to choose from, entertainment options that seemed limitless but somehow left him feeling emptier than before.

He described his coworkers—men from Mexico who sent money home to their families, a Syrian refugee who'd fled war, an ex-convict trying to rebuild his life. People whose stories humbled him, whose struggles made his own seem self-indulgent.

"I thought leaving would help me find myself," he said. "But all it did was show me that 'myself' was shaped by this place, these people, this way of life. I could learn new skills, see new things, but I couldn't become someone fundamentally different. The question wasn't who I was but whether I could accept being that person here, in this community, with all its limitations and expectations."

"And can you?" Emma asked. "Accept it, I mean?"

"I'm trying. The limitations feel different now—less like a cage and more like a framework. Structure that supports growth rather than preventing it. Maybe that's what growing up is—learning that boundaries can be *gut*, that tradition can coexist with innovation, that you don't have to reject everything to make room for yourself."

Emma understood exactly what he meant. It was the same tension she felt at the bakery—wanting to honor her grandmother's recipes while adding her own touches, respecting tradition while pushing gently at its edges.

"What about your peppermint bread?" Noah asked, as if reading her thoughts. "Are you going to introduce it at the Christmas market?"

"My father thinks it's too risky. That we should stick with proven items."

"But what do you think?"

Emma considered. "I think... I think there's room for both. Traditional *lebkuchen* for people who want what they've always known, and peppermint bread for people who are curious about something new. I don't have to choose between honoring the past and creating something of my own."

"No," Noah agreed. "You don't."

They sat in comfortable silence, the storm outside gradually lessening. Emma found herself acutely aware of Noah's presence—the way he moved, the timbre of his voice, the barely visible rise and fall of his chest as he breathed. This intimacy felt dangerous and precious at once, a stolen moment outside the normal rules and boundaries of their lives.

"I never forgot you," she admitted quietly. "I tried. I convinced myself I had. But every time I made *lebkuchen, I* thought about the first time I showed you my recipe. Every time I skated on the pond, I remembered holding your hand. Every Sunday hymn brought back the way our voices used to blend together."

"Emma—" His voice was rough with emotion.

"Let me finish." She took a breath, steadying herself. "I never forgot you, but I also couldn't forgive you. Those two things existed side by side—love and anger, memory and hurt. When Isaiah started courting me, I thought maybe that was for the best. Maybe I should choose someone I respect but don't love quite so much, someone who can't hurt me the way you did because I won't give him that power."

"That's not love. That's self-protection." Noah shifted to face her fully. "And I understand the impulse—*Gott* knows I've tried to protect myself too. But Emma, marriage should be more than just safety. It should be partnership and passion and the willingness to risk hurt because the alternative is a half-life."

"You're asking me to risk everything."

"I'm asking you to risk giving us a chance. To wait six months and see if I can prove I've changed. To not close doors before you're certain which path you want to walk." He paused. "But I'm also saying I understand if you can't. If the hurt was too deep, if trust is too broken, if Isaiah offers you what you need more than I ever could. I'll accept that. I'll step aside. But please, make that choice from strength, not fear."

Emma met his eyes across the flickering firelight. Everything in her wanted to say yes, to throw caution aside and risk her heart again. But she'd been burned before, badly enough that the scars still ached.

"I need time to think," she said finally. "Real time, not just this moment stolen from reality. When we go back to Miracle Creek, when the community and our families and all the expectations crash back in—I need to figure out what I want then, not just what I feel now."

Noah nodded slowly. "That's fair. That's more than fair, actually."

"But Noah?" Emma clutched the carved heart tighter. "Thank you. For being honest. For not pretending the past didn't happen or that everything can simply go back to how it was. For acknowledging that trust has to be rebuilt, not just assumed."

"It's the least I owe you."

They sat together as the storm gradually spent itself, keeping to safer topics—community news, the construction project, Emma's ideas for the bakery, Noah's plans for the widow's addition. The conversation flowed easily, natural and unforced, like slipping into well-worn clothes after a long day.

From time to time, Noah went to check on Clover, offering another peppermint each visit. The mare remained content, old and faithful, adjusting to the cabin's temporary shelter with quiet patience.

Emma found herself noticing small details—the way Noah's hands moved when he spoke about woodworking, precise and animated; the faint laugh lines around his eyes that hadn't been there before; the way he listened when she spoke, truly listened, as if her words mattered more than his own thoughts.

Eventually exhaustion caught up with them. Noah insisted Emma take the cot while he made a bed on the floor near the fire, piling up old blankets from a storage trunk. They lay in the darkness, the fire burning low, neither quite able to sleep despite their tiredness.

"Emma?" Noah's voice came soft from the floor.

"Yes?"

"Whatever you decide about us, about Isaiah, about your future—I want you to be happy. That's what I should have said five years ago instead of just disappearing. Your happiness matters more than my feelings, more than anyone's expectations. Don't forget that when you're making your choice."

Emma blinked back tears in the darkness, touched by the selflessness of the sentiment even as part of her wanted to shake him for being noble when she wanted him to fight for her. But maybe that was what maturity looked like—not passionate declarations but quiet respect for her agency, her right to choose her own path.

"Thank you," she whispered. *"Gut* night, Noah."

"Gut night, Emma."

She listened to his breathing slow and deepen as he fell asleep, but Emma lay awake for a long time, the carved heart tucked under her pillow, her mind spinning through possibilities and fears and the terrifying hope that maybe, just maybe, second chances were real.

* * *

By morning, the storm had passed entirely, leaving the world blanketed in pristine white. They walked back to town in silence, though they could have ridden freestyle—

like many Amish children, learning the saddle almost before they could walk. Yet neither wanted their stolen time together to end, even as the reality of expectation pressed in.

Clover trailed behind, steady and patient, as if aware of the fragile moment of honesty they had shared—a moment that would soon be overshadowed by judgment, questions, and consequences neither could foresee.

Isaiah was waiting when they reached the edge of town, his face thunderous.

"Where have you been?" His voice was cold, controlled. "The whole community has been searching. Your father is frantic, Emma."

"The sleigh broke," Emma explained, exhausted and too emotionally drained to care about appearances. "We took shelter in the old hunting cabin on the edge of Hope Valley until the storm passed. We're fine."

"Alone. All night." Isaiah's jaw clenched. "Do you have any idea what this looks like? What people will say?"

"Nothing happened," Noah said firmly. "We were stranded by weather, that's all."

"That's all?" Isaiah's laugh was bitter. "You've been back a month and already you're compromising Emma's reputation. This is exactly what everyone warned me about—that you'd disrupt things, cause problems, lead *gut* people astray."

"Isaiah—" Emma started, but he cut her off.

"The bishop will want to speak with both of you. Immediately." He turned on his heel and stalked toward the bishop's house, clearly expecting them to follow.

Emma and Noah exchanged a quick glance—hers tight with anxiety, his calm but resigned—before following Isaiah through the snow-covered streets.

Neighbors peered from windows and porches, faces a mix of concern, scandal, and perhaps a hint of sympathy.

Esther Coblentz remained on her porch, rocking quietly despite the cold, as if marking the passage of inevitable events.

The reckoning had arrived, and Emma had no way of knowing what it would cost them.

Chapter 9
The Bishop's Parlor

The bishop's parlor felt oppressively warm after the cold walk from the hunting cabin. Emma sat on a hard wooden chair, Noah standing beside her, while Isaiah paced near the window and Bishop Lapp studied them both with an expression that gave nothing away.

"Tell me exactly what happened," the bishop said, his voice calm but commanding absolute honesty.

Noah recounted the trip to gather evergreens, the broken sleigh runner, the approaching storm, and their decision to shelter in the cabin. His voice remained steady, factual, leaving nothing out but adding no unnecessary details either. Emma found herself grateful for his composure even as her own hands trembled in her lap.

When Noah finished, the bishop turned to Emma. "Do you confirm this account?"

"Yes. Everything happened exactly as Noah described. We had no choice—walking back in that storm would have been dangerous, possibly fatal."

"And yet," the bishop said carefully, "you were alone together, unchaperoned, for an entire night. You understand how this appears to the community?"

"I understand, but—"

"Perception matters as much as truth in these situations," Bishop Lapp interrupted. "Even if nothing improper occurred, the appearance of impropriety can damage reputations just as effectively."

"With respect, Sir," Noah said, his voice tight with controlled frustration, "would it have been better for us to freeze to death maintaining proper appearances?"

"Don't be flippant," the bishop snapped. "You know very well this could have been avoided with better judgment."

"What happens now?" Emma asked quietly.

The bishop settled back in his chair, fingers steepled in thought. "That depends on several factors. First, I need to hear from both of you: did anything inappropriate occur during your time alone together?"

"No," Noah said immediately.

"Nothing," Emma confirmed, heat flooding her cheeks at the implication.

"Very well. I believe you." The bishop's expression softened slightly. "However, the community's trust must be restored. Emma, your father is understandably concerned. Isaiah's family is understandably concerned. Steps must be taken."

"What kind of steps?" Emma felt dread pooling in her stomach.

The bishop turned to Isaiah, who'd stopped pacing and now stood with arms crossed, his expression carved from stone. "Isaiah, you've formally requested permission to court Emma. Do you still wish to pursue that course, given recent events?"

Isaiah's jaw worked as if chewing on bitter words. Finally: "I need time to consider. My feelings for Emma haven't changed, but I need to know she's committed to choosing a path forward within this community, not clinging to unsuitable attachments from the past."

His gaze landed pointedly on Noah.

The words cut, though Emma couldn't entirely blame him. She had been sending mixed signals for months, accepting attention while keeping her heart in reserve, waiting for something—or someone—else.

As if *Gott* had whispered to her heart: *wait. I have something better for you around the corner.* Or perhaps it was just hope speaking—hope against hope. Five long years of hope she had refused to acknowledge, lying dormant in her chest, ready to rise and protest at any other suitor who dared approach.

"Fair enough," the bishop said. "Emma, you will have to make a choice. Not today, not under pressure, but soon. The community needs clarity about your intentions. Are you open to Isaiah's courtship or not?"

"I need time to think—"

"You've had months to think," Bishop Lapp said, not unkindly but firmly. "Isaiah deserves an answer. He's been patient, has followed all proper protocols, has shown nothing but respect for you and your family. The question is simple: can you see yourself as his *fraa?* If not, you must tell him so he can move forward with his life."

Emma felt trapped, cornered, forced into a decision she wasn't ready to make. But the bishop was right—stringing Isaiah along wasn't fair to anyone.

"I'll give you until after Christmas," the bishop continued. "By then, you'll have answered Isaiah's courtship request one way or another."

"And Noah?" Emma asked, her voice barely above a whisper.

"Noah will complete his baptism preparations as planned. He'll continue leading the construction project for Widow Kauffman. He'll attend all community events and fulfill all obligations."

The bishop's eyes hardened. "But he will have no private contact with you until his baptism is complete and he's demonstrated his commitment to this community. No accidental meetings, no convenient excuses to be alone together. You will maintain proper distance."

"That's six months," Noah protested.

"Yes. Six months during which you can prove you're trustworthy, that you've truly changed, that you're capable of putting community welfare above personal desire." The bishop stood, signaling the meeting's end. "If you cannot accept these terms, you're free to leave again. But know that if you do, you won't be welcomed back a second time."

The ultimatum hung in the air, clear and uncompromising. Emma watched Noah's face, saw him wrestling with the unfairness of it, the way the bishop was stacking the deck in Isaiah's favor when he'd felt before that perhaps—just perhaps, the bishop was on true love's side. But what could they do? The bishop held all the power here, and defying him meant exile from everything they'd both been fighting to reclaim.

"I'll accept your terms," Noah said finally, defeat evident in his slumped shoulders.

"*Gut.*" The bishop turned to Emma. "Your father is waiting at home. I suggest you go to him and explain what happened. He deserves to hear it from you."

Emma nodded numbly and stood, her legs unsteady beneath her. As she moved toward the door, she glanced back at Noah. Their eyes met for a moment—his filled with apology and regret, hers with confusion and something that might have been goodbye.

Then she was outside in the cold morning air, walking home alone, the carved wooden heart still in her pocket feeling heavier with each step.

* * *

The walk home took fifteen minutes, but it felt like hours. Emma's mind raced through the conversation with the bishop, through all the ways the situation had spun out of control, through the impossible choice she'd been given.

She had until Christmas to decide her future. Two weeks to determine whether she'd choose safety with Isaiah or the terrifying possibility of Noah. Except it wasn't even that simple—Noah wouldn't be an option for six months, and by then she'd likely be married to Isaiah or have firmly closed that door forever.

The injustice of it burned in her chest. Noah was being punished for circumstances largely beyond his control, while Isaiah was being rewarded for simply being present and persistent. Life wasn't fair—Emma had always known that—but understanding it didn't make it easier to accept.

Her father was indeed waiting when she arrived home, his face lined with worry that shifted to relief and then anger in rapid succession.

"Emma, *mei dochder!* Thank the Lord you're safe. Where have you been?" *Datt* pulled her into a brief, fierce hug before holding her at arm's length, searching her face. "The whole town has been looking for you. When the storm hit and you didn't come home, we feared the worst. Isaiah told us you were back—"

"I'm sorry, *Datt.* The sleigh broke, and Noah and I had to shelter in the old hunting cabin out by Hope Valley. We're both fine."

"Alone? All night?" Michael's expression hardened. "Emma, how could you be so foolish? Your reputation—"

"Will survive," Emma said, more sharply than intended. "I'm sorry for worrying you, but we had no choice. Would you rather I'd frozen to death to preserve appearances? That Noah's horse got injured because—"

She glanced at her mother, just entered the room, searching for support from her, but found only worry etched into her brow, nodding slightly to her father's words.

"Don't be dramatic. I'm saying you should have been more careful, more aware of the weather, more—" said Michael.

"More what, *Datt?*" Emma felt weeks of suppressed frustration bubbling over. "More obedient? More cautious? More willing to sacrifice my own judgment to avoid gossip?"

Datt looked stunned by her outburst. Emma was never the rebellious one, never the child who questioned or challenged. That had always been her elder brother, Stephen's role. Now much calmer, and married with two *kinder* of his own.

"I'm not a child anymore," Emma continued, her voice shaking but determined. "I'm twenty-two years old. I run a successful bakery that employs people. I make decisions every day that affect our family's income. But I'm expected to defer to everyone else when it comes to my own life, my own future?"

"Emma, that's not—"

"Isaiah wants to court me, and everyone thinks it's a *gut* match. Maybe it is. He's kind and stable and would be a *gut* provider. But no one has asked me what *I* want. Not you, not *Mamm*, not Bishop Lapp, Bishop Weaver, any of the elders, not even Isaiah himself. I'm just expected to smile and accept and be grateful for the opportunity."

"Because it IS a gut opportunity!" Her *datt's* voice rose to match hers. "Isaiah is the son of a bishop. That match would secure your future, give you status and security. What more could you want?"

"Love," Emma said simply. "Partnership. Someone who sees me as more than a convenient wife, more than a way to fulfill community expectations."

"And you think Noah Albrecht can give you that?" Her father's laugh was bitter. "A man who abandoned you once already? Who comes back with no clear plans, no property of his own, nothing but promises that he's changed? Talk is cheap!"

"Maybe. Maybe not." Emma met her father's eyes squarely. "But shouldn't that be my choice to make? My risk to take?"

The silence stretched between them, heavy with years of unspoken expectations and suppressed desires on both sides.

Finally, Michael sighed, his shoulders sagging as if the weight of worry had aged him suddenly. "I just want you to be safe, Emma. Happy and safe. That's all. That's all I and your mother want."

Mamm nodded, the strings on her prayer *kapp* bouncing slightly with every reassuring nod.

"I know, *Mamm*.... *Datt*. I know you do." Emma's anger ebbed, leaving only exhaustion in its place. "But safe isn't always the same as happy. And sometimes—" She thought of Widow Kauffman's story, of choices made from fear instead of courage. This story had been told to her too. "Sometimes the safe choice is the one you regret most."

Her *datt* opened his mouth to respond, but her *mamm* ushered Emma toward the kitchen to eat some hot soup, throwing her husband a look that clearly said: Leave this alone for now. You've said your piece.

Emma allowed herself to be shepherded away, grateful for her mother's intervention even as she felt the weight of her father's disappointment following her like a shadow.

* * *

The next few days passed in a blur of work and whispers. Emma threw herself into bakery preparations for the Christmas market, spending long hours perfecting recipes and managing inventory. The work helped, gave her hands something to do and her mind something to focus on besides the impossible choice looming ahead.

The Christmas market committee met three days after the snowstorm incident. Emma arrived at the community hall to find it already full, families gathered to discuss booth assignments, layout plans, and the dozens of details that went into their biggest annual event.

Isaiah was there, of course, clipboard in hand, presenting his traditional market layout with the confidence of someone who'd never been told his plans might be questioned.

Emma sat with the younger members of the committee—Ruth Stoltzfus and Rebecca Lapp —women who'd grown up with her and shared her cautious hopes for gentle innovation. Deborah Peachey, though a relative newcomer to town, was also on the Committee due to her status as Miracle Creek's schoolteacher.

"As you can see," Isaiah explained, pointing to his hand-drawn map, "we'll maintain the same basic structure we've used successfully for years. Familiarity is important for our customers, both English and Amish. They know where to find what they're looking for. Change for its own sake serves no purpose."

Several older committee members nodded approvingly. Emma felt Rebecca nudge her encouragingly.

"While tradition is certainly valuable," Emma said, standing despite her shaking hands, "I wonder if we might also consider adding something new this year. A small innovation section for crafts and foods that honor our heritage while inviting fresh interest."

The room erupted in murmurs. Some faces showed interest; others skepticism or outright disapproval.

"What kind of innovation?" Bishop Lapp asked, his tone neutral but his eyes sharp.

"New recipes that use traditional techniques—like my peppermint bread, which several customers have expressed interest in. New craft designs that modernize traditional patterns without abandoning them. Things that might draw younger customers or *Englisch* tourists looking for something beyond the usual offerings."

"And who would run this innovation section?" Isaiah's voice was cold, though his expression remained pleasant.

"I would," Emma said, forcing herself to meet his eyes. "And perhaps others who have ideas they'd like to test. Noah Albrecht, for instance, has woodworking skills from his time away that blend traditional Amish craftsmanship with contemporary design. His work could attract attention."

The mention of Noah's name sent fresh murmurs through the room. Emma saw her father's expression darken, saw the bishop's eyes narrow slightly.

"Noah Albrecht's participation would be...

premature," Bishop Lapp said carefully. "He hasn't yet proven his commitment to community standards. Including him in our most visible public event might send the wrong message."

"With respect, Bishop," Emma pressed on despite knowing she was pushing boundaries, "isn't the construction project for Widow Kauffman also a public demonstration? If he's trusted to lead that, why not trust him to contribute his skills to the market?"

"The construction project serves internal community needs," Isaiah interjected smoothly. "The Christmas market presents our community to outsiders. The standards are necessarily different."

Emma wanted to argue further, to point out the hypocrisy of the distinction, but she felt Deborah's warning touch on her arm. She was already on thin ice; pushing harder might crack it completely.

"I still think an innovation section has merit," Emma said instead, moderating her tone. "Even without Noah's participation. It could bring in additional revenue, attract new customers, show that our community respects tradition while remaining relevant."

The bishop considered this. "I'm willing to allow a small trial section. Emma, you may have three tables in a designated area—not central, but visible enough to gauge interest. You'll be responsible for curating the items and ensuring they meet community standards. Nothing too worldly or flashy, understood?"

"Yes, Bishop. Thank you." Emma sat down, relief and disappointment mixing together. She'd won something, but far less than she'd hoped for.

"Well done!" whispered Deborah.

The meeting continued, but Emma barely heard the

rest of it. Her mind was already spinning with plans—what recipes to showcase, which crafters to approach, how to design the space to be inviting without being showy.

After the meeting adjourned, Isaiah approached her, his expression unreadable.

"That was bold of you," he said. "Speaking up like that."

"I was simply sharing an idea I thought had value."

"Defending Noah had value?" Isaiah's voice dropped lower. "Emma, I need to know—are you still carrying feelings for him? Because if you are, I deserve honesty about that."

Emma met his eyes, seeing genuine pain beneath his controlled exterior. Isaiah wasn't a bad man. He didn't deserve to be strung along while she figured out her own heart.

"I don't know what I feel," she admitted. "About Noah, about you, about my future. Everything is confused right now."

"Then let me help clarify things." Isaiah's voice softened. "I care for you, Emma. I have for years. I would be a *gut* husband—faithful, hardworking, devoted. I would respect you, provide for you, honor you as my wife. That's not passion or wild romance, but it's real. It's lasting. The candle that burns steady burns longest ... " He paused, letting his metaphor sink in. "Can Noah offer you that? Even if he stays this time, can you ever fully trust him not to leave again?"

The question struck at Emma's deepest fears. "I don't know," she whispered.

"You have until Christmas to decide about my courtship." Isaiah's hand briefly touched her shoulder—a rare physical gesture that felt both comforting and confining. "I hope you'll choose wisely. Not just for yourself, but for both our families, for the community that's counting on us."

He walked away, leaving Emma standing alone in the emptying hall, the weight of expectations pressing down like stones on her chest.

* * *

That night, Emma sat at her small desk in her bedroom, the carved wooden heart Noah had given her resting beside the star and a half-written letter to no one in particular. She'd started keeping a journal after the snowstorm, trying to sort through her tangled feelings by putting them on paper.

> *Isaiah is right that he can offer stability, security, a clearly defined future. No uncertainty, no risk of abandonment. That should be enough. That should be everything a sensible woman wants.*
>
> *But when I think about spending the rest of my life as Isaiah's wife, I feel... nothing. No excitement, no joy, just a kind of resigned acceptance. Is that what marriage should feel like?*
>
> *Noah makes me feel alive. Even when we're arguing, even when he's frustrating me, even when he's reminding me of how badly he hurt me—I feel SOMETHING. Anger, joy, confusion, hope. A whole spectrum of emotions I've been trying to suppress for five years.*
>
> *The bishop says I have to choose. Two weeks to decide about Isaiah's courtship, six months before Noah completes baptism and could potentially court me properly. But what if Isaiah won't wait six months?*

What if I turn him down now, wait for Noah, and then Noah leaves again? I'll have thrown away security for nothing.

Is that what faith is—choosing hope over certainty, possibility over safety? Or is it just foolishness, the same naivety that got me hurt the first time?

I wish Mammi were still alive. She'd know what to do. Or at least she'd tell me to stop overthinking and trust my heart. But what if my heart is lying? What if what feels right is actually a terrible mistake? Noah hurt me before...

Emma set down her pen, no closer to answers than when she'd started. The wooden heart caught the lamplight, its carefully carved surface glowing warm. Noah had spent hours on this, thinking of her, working through his own tangled feelings with his hands.

She picked it up, tracing the forget-me-nots, feeling the smoothness of wood worn by his touch. This was a promise, of sorts. A declaration that she'd mattered during those five years of silence, proof that she'd never been forgotten even if she'd been left behind.

But promises carved in wood were still just words. Actions mattered more. And Noah's most significant action had been leaving.

Could people really change? Could five years transform someone fundamentally, or did they just learn to hide their same old patterns beneath a more mature exterior?

Emma didn't know. And that uncertainty was its own kind of agony.

She tucked the heart into her desk drawer, buried beneath papers where it couldn't watch her with its silent accusations and impossible hopes. Then she blew out the lamp and climbed into bed, knowing sleep would be elusive but trying anyway.

Tomorrow the work on Widow Kauffman's addition would continue. Tomorrow she'd see Noah from a distance, maintaining the proper separation the bishop demanded. Tomorrow she'd count down another day toward the deadline hanging over her head.

Two weeks until Christmas. Two weeks until she had to choose a path forward.

It felt like both forever and nowhere near enough time.

Chapter 10
The Handcrafted Gift

The Christmas market preparations consumed Emma's waking hours over the next few days. She rose before dawn to bake experimental batches of peppermint bread, tweaking the recipe until it achieved the perfect balance between familiar and new. By day, she managed the regular bakery business. By night, she planned her innovation section with meticulous care, knowing that eyes would be watching for any excuse to call it a failure.

Joanna and even Deborah helped, their enthusiasm buoying Emma when doubt threatened to overwhelm her. They gathered crafts from younger community members —quilts with modern color combinations, wooden toys with contemporary designs, preserves in creative flavor combinations that still used traditional methods.

"This is going to be wonderful," Deborah said, examining a quilt that used traditional patterns but arranged them in an unexpected spiral. "People will love it."

"Or they'll hate it and the bishop will shut us down," Emma countered, anxiety making her voice sharper than intended.

"Have faith." Deborah squeezed her hand. The flame-haired schoolteacher was fast becoming her best friend. "Not everything new is bad. Even the elders must see that."

But Emma wasn't so sure. She caught whispers

wherever she went—about her night alone with Noah, about her bold proposal at the committee meeting, about her rejection of Isaiah's courtship becoming inevitable. The community was watching, judging, waiting to see which way she'd fall.

The market was set for the Saturday before Christmas, which gave Emma just days to finalize everything. Days until her innovation section would be tested publicly. Days until she had to give Isaiah her answer.

* * *

The night before the market, Emma was working late at the bakery when someone knocked on the locked door. Through the frosted glass, she saw Noah's silhouette.

She shouldn't answer. The bishop's restrictions were clear. But her feet carried her to the door anyway, her hand turning the lock before wisdom could intervene.

"I know I shouldn't be here," Noah said immediately, not stepping inside. "But I made something for your market section. I'll leave it on the doorstep if you'd rather not—"

"Come in." Emma glanced down the street—empty, thank *Gott*—and pulled him quickly inside. "Just for a moment. My father is not here."

Noah entered carrying a wooden crate. He set it carefully on the counter and pulled back the cloth covering. Inside lay a beautiful display stand, carved with intricate snowflake patterns that caught the lamplight and seemed to shimmer.

Emma's breath caught. "Noah, it's beautiful."

"It's functional too," he said, his voice warm with pride in his work. "See how it has different levels? You can display breads here, smaller items like cookies here, and the design draws the eye upward." He demonstrated, his hands moving with confident grace. "I thought about your peppermint bread, about how you wanted to honor tradition while creating something new. This does that—traditional Amish joinery and design principles, but with a contemporary aesthetic that might appeal to English customers."

Emma ran her fingers over the smooth wood, feeling the care in every joint and curve. "This is exactly what I needed. How did you know?"

"I pay attention." Noah's eyes met hers. "I always have, even when I shouldn't have been watching you."

The admission hung between them, loaded with longing and frustration at the forced separation.

"The bishop would be angry if he knew you were here," Emma said, though she made no move to hurry him out. "My father too."

"I know. But some things are worth the risk." Noah pulled another piece from the crate—a small carved sign that read "New Traditions" in elegant script. "For your section. If you want it."

"I want it." Emma traced the letters with her finger. "Thank you, Noah. This means more than you know."

"I should go before someone sees my buggy outside."

"Noah, wait." Emma caught his hand impulsively. "Thank you. Not just for this, but for—for everything. For coming back. For trying. For giving me something beautiful to remember you by if—" Her voice caught. "If things don't work out the way we hope."

Noah's fingers tightened on hers. "Emma, I need you to know something. Whether you choose Isaiah or choose to wait for me or choose some third path I can't imagine —I won't regret coming back. Being near you these past weeks, even from a distance, even with all the restrictions and judgment—it's been worth it. You're worth it."

"Don't," Emma whispered, tears threatening. "Don't make this harder."

"I'm sorry." He released her hand, stepping back. "I'll go. Use the stand or don't, as you think best. I just wanted you to have it either way."

After he left, Emma stood alone in the quiet bakery, surrounded by the tools of her trade and Noah's gifts. The display stand would be perfect for the market. But using it meant publicly declaring their connection, accepting his help, essentially choosing sides in a conflict she'd tried to avoid.

She ran her hand over the carved snowflakes one more time, then made her decision. She'd use it. She'd honor the gift and the giver, regardless of consequences.

Some things were worth the risk.

* * *

Market day arrived with clear skies and bitter cold. Emma rose at three in the morning to begin final preparations, loading her wagon with breads and pastries and the new peppermint loaves she'd spent weeks perfecting. The display stand went in last, wrapped carefully to protect its delicate carvings.

The market grounds were already bustling when she arrived at dawn. Vendors claimed their spaces, stringing lights and arranging wares. The air smelled of wood smoke and cinnamon, pine boughs and hope.

Emma's "New Traditions" section occupied three tables near the main entrance—not central as she'd wanted, but visible enough. She arranged Noah's display stand as the centerpiece, then carefully positioned her peppermint loaves on its graduated levels. The effect was striking—traditional food presented in a way that invited curiosity.

Around her breads, she arranged the other items she'd curated: Deborah's modern-colored quilts, Martha's jam in unusual flavor combinations, Ruth's preserves with hand-lettered labels. Everything honored tradition while reaching toward innovation.

"It looks wonderful," her *mamm* said, appearing with coffee and encouragement. "You've done something real special here, Emma."

"I hope people think so." Emma accepted the coffee gratefully. "I hope this wasn't a terrible mistake."

"Even if it is, mistakes are how we learn and grow. Your *grossmami* taught you that."

Emma thought of her grandmother's patient instruction, the way she'd encouraged Emma's small rebellions with the *lebkuchen* recipe. Would she be proud of this bolder step? Or would she counsel more caution?

The market opened at eight. Within minutes, Emma's section drew curious customers—both Amish families and *Englisch* tourists. The display stand caught eyes immediately, its elegant design marking the space as special.

"What's this?" an *Englisch* woman asked, picking up a peppermint loaf. "I've never seen this flavor before."

"It's a new recipe," Emma explained, her practiced pitch smooth despite her nerves. "Traditional Amish techniques with a contemporary twist. The base honors my grandmother's *lebkuchen* recipe, but the peppermint adds something fresh for modern tastes."

"I love that idea—honoring the past while moving forward." The woman bought three loaves. "My book club will adore these."

More customers followed—some skeptical, many intrigued, all curious. Emma found herself explaining her philosophy over and over: tradition and innovation weren't enemies but partners, each making the other stronger.

By noon, she'd sold more than half her inventory. The innovation section buzzed with activity while some of the traditional booths stood quiet. Emma felt vindicated but also anxious—success meant she'd proven her point, but it also meant standing out, drawing attention, potentially threatening people who valued sameness over change.

Isaiah appeared during the afternoon lull, his expression unreadable as he surveyed Emma's nearly-empty tables.

"You've done well," he said, surprising her with the admission. "Better than anyone expected."

"Thank you." Emma wiped her hands on her apron, suddenly self-conscious.

"I see you're using Noah Albrecht's display stand." Isaiah's tone remained neutral, but Emma heard the unspoken question.

She was not sure how he heard it was Noah's but there was no point in denying it.

"He offered it. The craftsmanship is excellent—people have been asking about it all day."

"I'm sure they have." Isaiah picked up one of the few remaining peppermint loaves, studying it. "Emma, I need to know—have you made your decision about my courtship?"

The question, asked here in public space with people milling nearby, felt like an ambush. But perhaps that was Isaiah's intent—to force an answer while Emma was flushed with success, before she could retreat into uncertainty.

"I have," Emma said quietly, her heart pounding.

"And?"

"Isaiah, you're a *gut* man. You'd make someone a wonderful husband. But that someone isn't me." The words came easier than she'd expected, carrying the weight of truth finally acknowledged. "I can't accept your courtship. I'm sorry."

Isaiah's face remained carefully composed, but Emma saw hurt flash through his eyes before he controlled it. "Because of Noah."

"Because I don't love you the way a wife should love her husband. You deserve someone who does. I've prayed about it and—"

"Love can grow in marriage. Our grandparents didn't marry for love—they married for practical reasons and learned to love each other over time."

"Maybe. But I can't promise I'd ever feel more than respect and affection. That's not fair to either of us."

Isaiah set down the bread, his movements precise. "My father won't be pleased. Your father won't be pleased. This will complicate things considerably."

"I know. But it's the honest answer you asked for."

"And Noah? Are you waiting for him? Because six months is a long time, Emma. He could change his mind. He could leave again. You could end up alone. A spinster."

"That's possible." Emma met his eyes steadily. "But I'd rather risk that than marry someone I don't love while hoping Noah might still be available." She thought of Widow Kaufmann always wondering what could have been. "You deserve better than to be someone's safe second choice."

Isaiah nodded slowly, accepting if not agreeing. "I

wish you well, Emma. I truly do. But I think you're making a mistake."

He walked away through the crowd, his posture stiff with wounded pride. Emma watched him go, feeling both relief and sadness. She'd hurt him, which she'd never wanted. But staying silent would have hurt him worse in the long run.

"That took courage," Deborah said, appearing at Emma's elbow. "Everyone will be talking."

But Deborah's face also looked relieved.

"Let them talk." Emma straightened her shoulders. "I'm done making decisions based on what everyone else thinks I should do."

The rest of the market passed in a blur. Emma sold out of peppermint bread by four o'clock and took orders for more. Her innovation section was declared a success by even skeptical observers. The bishop stopped by, his expression thoughtful as he examined the display.

"You've done well," he said simply. "This honors our traditions while showing wisdom about changing times. Well done, Emma."

The praise, coming from him, felt like vindication.

As she was loading her empty wagon, Noah appeared —keeping a respectful distance, though his smile was warm. Clover trailed beside him, her breath curling into the crisp air. Emma resisted the impulse to step closer, to pat the mare's velvet nose, knowing that even that small act would draw her nearer to Noah. Instead, she smiled at Clover and whispered her name softly.

Noah's eyes warmed at the sight. "She remembers you," he said, a hint of amusement in his voice. "I heard you sold out. Congratulations."

Emma busied herself with the wagon straps, trying to

steady her heartbeat. "Your display stand helped. People loved it—several asked if you make them for sale."

He ducked his head a little, half a grin tugging at his mouth. "Maybe I should. Seems folks here appreciate *gut,* sturdy work."

"Sturdy," Emma repeated, her voice gentler than she meant it to be. "You always were good at making things that last."

Their eyes met for a heartbeat too long. Around them, the market hummed—the thud of boots on packed snow, the clatter of horses' hooves, the murmured rhythm of familiar voices—but it all seemed to fade beneath the weight of what wasn't being said.

"Maybe I should." Noah's eyes held hers. "I also heard you spoke with Isaiah."

News traveled fast. "I turned down his courtship."

Something flickered in Noah's expression—hope mixed with concern. "Because of me?"

"Because of me," Emma corrected. "Because I needed to stop letting other people decide my future. Whatever happens between us—or doesn't—that was the right choice."

"Emma—"

"Don't." She held up a hand, stopping whatever declaration he'd been about to make. "You still have six months of baptism preparation. I need that time too—to figure out who I am separate from everyone's expectations. We can't build anything real if we don't first build ourselves into people capable of sustaining it."

Noah absorbed this, then nodded slowly. "That's fair. That's wise, actually."

"Wisdom is new for me," Emma admitted with a small laugh. "I'm trying it out."

They stood in the winter afternoon, the market noise fading around them, both aware they'd crossed some threshold. Emma had closed one door. But the other remained open, leading somewhere uncertain but possible.

"Six months," Noah said. "I'll use them well. I promise."

"So will I."

Then Emma exhaled, pulling her shawl tighter. "You should go," she murmured. "If people see us talking too long, they'll start to wonder."

Noah nodded, but didn't move right away. "Let them wonder a little," he said softly. Then, after a pause: "I'm glad you're all right, Emma."

Her answering smile was small but real. "You too, Noah."

Clover flicked her ears, snorting as if in approval, before Noah led her away down the lane. Emma watched until the sleigh bell's distant jingle faded into silence, the echo of his voice—and the memory of the storm— lingering long after he was gone.

She'd made her choice—not Noah specifically, but possibility over safety, hope over certainty. Whatever came next, at least she'd chosen it herself.

That had to count for something.

Chapter 11
The Unfinished Carving

Noah sat on a log by the frozen pond the night before Christmas Eve, his breath fogging in the bitter cold.

The pond stretched before him, ice gleaming under the moon. This place held so many memories—summer afternoons with Emma, winter skating parties, the promises they'd whispered believing they'd last forever. Coming here felt like visiting a shrine to who he'd been, who he'd hoped to become.

"You look troubled."

Noah turned to find Widow Kauffman approaching carefully across the snow, her cane finding purchase on the icy path.

"Just thinking," Noah said, standing to offer his arm for support. "What are you doing out so late?"

"Saw you from my window. Recognized the shape of someone carrying heavy thoughts." She settled onto a fallen log, patting the space beside her. "Sit. Tell an old woman what weighs on your heart."

It reminded him of their previous conversation.

Noah sat, surprised by the invitation to honesty. He shrugged. "Emma."

The widow was quiet for a long moment, her eyes distant with memory. "Fear is a terrible foundation for decisions. It keeps us safe but small. *Gott* wants more for us than just safety."

"I followed your advice. I told her I feel. But the bishop says—"

"The bishop means well. But remember what I also said, he's not infallible." The widow's expression was kind but firm. "He wants to protect the community, which is *gut*. But sometimes protection becomes control, and control becomes fear dressed up as faithfulness."

Noah absorbed this, hearing the warning beneath her words.

"What are you afraid of, Noah?" the widow asked. "Really afraid of, under all the talk about baptism and community acceptance?"

The question struck deeper than he expected. Noah stared at the floor, the words slow to form. "That I'll hurt Emma again. That I'll fail at building a life here. That whatever's broken in me—the part that made me run before—will make me run again. Because I'm not sure I have the kind of faith that believes impossible things can be made whole again."

The widow studied him for a long moment, then nodded slowly. "And what if you *are* capable?" she said, her voice soft but steady. "What if faith isn't about being certain, but about hoping *despite* uncertainty? About trusting—obeying—even when you can't see the way forward?"

She moved toward the door, pulling her shawl around her shoulders. "You remember what the man said to Jesus—the one with the sick boy? *'I believe; Lord, help my unbelief.'* Do you know what that means, Noah? It means acknowledging the humanity in us all—the part that wrestles, that doubts, yet still reaches toward *Gott* anyway."

Her eyes glimmered with quiet conviction. "You've been walking through the valley of the shadow these past five years. But what does the Psalm promise? *'Yea, though I walk through the valley of the shadow of death, Thou art with me.*"' She laid a hand gently on his arm. "Where can any of us go from His Spirit? Even in your running, He was there. Always."

She smiled faintly. "So be like that doubting man of faith—paradoxical though it seems—and cry out, *'I believe; Lord, help my unbelief.'* Come to Jesus just as you are, Noah. That's all He ever asks."

With that, she turned and walked out into the snow, leaving Noah alone in the moonlight—and in the weight of her words.

Something in him broke open then. All the walls he'd built, all the justifications and quiet anger, crumpled like thawing ice. Noah sank to his knees in the wet snow and spoke to Gott—*truly* spoke—for the first time in years. The words came haltingly at first, then freely, like a dam giving way to a long-dammed river.

When at last he lifted his head, the moon had climbed high above the silent fields, washing everything in silver light. The road ahead was still uncertain, the questions still many.

But for the first time since returning to Miracle Creek, Noah felt ready to walk it.

* * *

The next day, Noah worked on Widow Kauffman's addition with renewed energy. The project was nearly complete—just finish work remaining before they could declare it ready for winter. The men worked with practiced efficiency, each knowing his role, the construction a kind of dance they'd perfected over weeks together.

"You've done *gut* work here, *mei soh,*" Gideon said during a water break, the first real compliment he'd given Noah since his return. "The widow will be warm and safe through the winter."

"We all did it together," Noah deflected, but warmth spread through his chest at his father's approval.

"You led it. That matters." Gideon's hand briefly squeezed Noah's shoulder. "Your mother's proud. I'm... I'm learning to be."

The admission, painfully honest, made Noah's throat tight. "I know I have more to prove."

"You've already proven plenty. The rest is just time— showing that today's Noah is tomorrow's Noah too. Consistency. That's what I'm waiting to see."

"I'll show you," Noah promised. "I'm not leaving again, *Datt.* This is home. It always was."

His *datt's* stern features softened into a smile. "*Gut,* because Clover and Shep would sure miss you. They've gotten used to having you around the place."

It was his *datt's* way of saying what didn't need to be said aloud—that he loved his son, and would miss him fiercely if he ever left again.

They returned to work, but something had shifted between them—not forgiveness exactly, but the beginning of it. The beginning of trust rebuilt one careful step at a time.

That evening, as Noah put away tools, Emma appeared with Deborah and Joanna, bringing dinner for the work crew. Emma and Noah maintained proper distance, barely speaking, but their eyes met across the construction site—hers questioning, his steady with newfound certainty.

Noah saw Michael watching them, his expression

thoughtful rather than hostile. Perhaps Emma's decision about Isaiah had changed how her father saw Noah, or perhaps the weeks of consistent work had earned grudging respect. Either way, the hostility had softened into something closer to wary acceptance.

After the crew departed, Noah stayed behind to do a final check. Emma stayed too, helping the other girls clean up dishes but moving closer to Noah as the others drifted away.

Noah met her gaze. "I've come to realize something," he said quietly. "Hope isn't the absence of doubt—it's the choice to believe in possibility *despite* doubt. To take the risk, even knowing everything that could go wrong."

Emma's eyes softened. "You're talking about more than your walk with *Gott.*"

"I'm talking about *us,*" he said, his voice barely above a whisper. "About choosing to believe we can rebuild what was broken. Even when there are no guarantees— just my word, and what you can see in my eyes." He held her gaze steadily. "That I love you. I always have. And I'm willing to risk everything for that. And I hope you would too. Because the alternative—safety without possibility—is worse than uncertainty."

"Noah, I—"

"You don't have to say anything right now," he said softly, interrupting her. "The bishop asked for six months, and you deserve that time. I just need you to know that I've made my choice."

He took a slow breath, his gaze steady on hers. "I've always known it was you. I don't even know if love is something you *choose*—I think sometimes your heart just decides, and mine decided a long time ago. It's always been you."

He exhaled, a small, weary smile touching his lips. "But whether you choose to have me back or not, whether you take that risk, I'm staying. I'm building a life here. I'm becoming someone worth choosing. And I hope that when those six months are up… you'll take that risk."

Emma's eyes glistened with unshed tears. "Noah, I need to tell you something." She took a breath, steadying herself. "When you left five years ago, something broke in me. I convinced myself I'd moved on, but I was really just hiding from the hurt. When you came back, all that pain resurfaced and I didn't know how to handle it. I tried to choose safety with Isaiah because safety felt better than risking my heart again."

Noah listened intently, not interrupting.

"But watching you work and try and prove yourself— you've shown me that people can change. That the Noah who left isn't the same as the Noah who came back. And I've changed too. I'm not the girl who needed someone else to define her future. I'm a woman who can stand on her own, make her own choices, risk her own heart."

"What are you saying?" Noah's voice was rough with emotion.

"I'm saying I don't want to wait six months. Life is too uncertain and too precious to waste time being careful when we could be living." Emma pulled the carved heart from her pocket. "You gave me this as a reminder that you never forgot me. I'm giving it back as a promise—I'm not going to forget you either. When you complete your baptism, when you're ready to court someone properly, I'll be here. Waiting. Choosing possibility over safety."

"Emma." Noah's eyes glistened with tears he didn't bother hiding. "Are you sure? Because once you say this,

I'm holding you to it. I'm not letting go again."

"I'm sure." And she was—more certain than she'd been of anything in years.

Isaiah appeared then, his expression carefully neutral. "Emma. Noah. Merry Christmas."

"Merry Christmas, Isaiah," Emma said, meaning it genuinely.

Isaiah's eyes moved between them, reading what was unspoken. "I hope you'll both be very happy together. When the time comes."

The grace in his words touched Emma deeply. "Thank you. That means more than you know."

Isaiah nodded and moved away, leaving them alone again.

"Six months," Noah said. "I'll use them to become someone worthy of that promise."

"You already are," Emma replied. "But I'll use them too—to build the bakery, to grow into myself, to be ready for whatever comes next."

They parted then, returning to their respective families, but the connection between them felt solid now, real, something they could both trust and build toward.

Christmas Eve had never felt more magical.

* * *

Later that night, Emma stood at her bedroom window watching snow fall over Miracle Creek. The wooden heart sat on her windowsill, catching moonlight. In six months, Noah would complete his baptism. In six months, they could begin courting openly, building toward a future together.

Six months felt both eternal and fleeting. But for the first time since Noah's return, Emma felt at peace with the waiting. They were both works in progress, both becoming people capable of sustaining the relationship they wanted. The time apart was necessary, valuable even.

She thought of Widow Kauffman's story, of choosing safety and always wondering what might have been. Emma had chosen differently—chosen risk and possibility and hope that felt dangerous but alive.

Outside, the snow continued to fall, covering old tracks, making everything new. Tomorrow was Christmas. Tomorrow they'd celebrate with family and community. Tomorrow they'd wake to a world transformed by winter's patient work.

But tonight, Emma let herself simply feel grateful—for second chances, for courage found, for love that had survived five years of silence and returned stronger for the testing.

The future remained uncertain. But uncertainty, she was learning, was just another word for possibility.

And possibility felt like the best Christmas gift of all.

Epilogue
Christmas Full Circle

The Following December

Emma stood in their living room—hers and Noah's—arranging the wooden star and heart on the shelf with careful reverence. The same pieces Noah had carved a year ago, but now displayed in their home, their sanctuary built together through months of patient waiting and careful building.

Pippin, their rescued stray cat, wound around her ankles, purring contentedly. The house was warm despite the winter cold outside, the smell of fresh bread and Christmas spices filling every corner. Tomorrow they'd host both families for Christmas dinner—the Masts and Albrechts united by marriage and forgiveness and the slow healing that came from choosing hope over fear.

"Is this how my *fraa* welcomes me home?" Noah's voice came from the doorway, warmth and teasing mixed together in the tone she'd grown to treasure. "Standing at the mantel looking beautiful while I freeze outside bringing in firewood?"

Emma turned, smiling at her husband of four months. The wedding had been in August, after Noah completed his baptism and proved to the community—and himself—that he was staying for good. It had been a simple ceremony, attended by everyone who'd doubted and judged and eventually accepted their unlikely reunion.

"Your presence adds to the ambiance," Emma

countered, moving to help him stack wood by the fireplace.

"Everything you do requires concentration. It's one of the things I love about you—the way you approach each task like it's an art form." Noah brushed flour from her cheek, his touch still capable of sending shivers through her even after months of marriage. "How's the baking for tomorrow?"

"Done. Well, mostly done. I might make one more batch of peppermint bread—"

"Emma." Noah captured her hands, stilling their nervous movement. "Everything doesn't have to be perfect. Our families love us. They'll love whatever food you serve."

"I know. I just want it to be special."

"It will be. Because we're together. Because both our families will be under one roof celebrating not just Christmas but everything we've built this year. That's already more special than any amount of baking can make it."

Emma leaned into him, letting his solid presence ground her anxiety. He was right, of course. The food mattered less than the gathering, the coming together of families that had once been skeptical but now supported them wholeheartedly.

"I have something to tell you," Emma said, her heart racing with nerves and excitement. "A Christmas gift, though it won't arrive until summer."

Noah pulled back to look at her, confusion and hope warring in his expression. "What do you mean?"

"I'm expecting. The baby should arrive in July."

Joy exploded across Noah's face like sunrise. He swept Emma into his arms, laughing and spinning her around the living room while Pippin meowed indignantly and fled to higher ground.

"Emma! That's—you're—we're going to have a baby?" Noah's voice cracked with emotion as he set her down gently, his hands immediately moving to her still-flat stomach. "Are you sure? How long have you known?"

"The midwife, Sarah Mathews, confirmed it last week. I've been waiting for the right moment to tell you."

"This is the right moment. This is the perfect moment." Noah knelt before her, his hands reverent on her belly. "Hello in there. I'm your father, and I promise I'll be here for you. I'll teach you woodworking and how to skate on the frozen creek and—" His voice broke. "I'll never leave you. Either of you. This is where I belong."

Emma's eyes filled with tears—happy ones, for once, instead of the anxious tears that had marked so much of the past year. "

"I know you won't leave," Emma said, running her fingers through Noah's hair as he knelt before her. "You've proven that a hundred times over."

"And I'll keep proving it." He stood, pulling her close again. "Every day for the rest of our lives."

They stood together in their home, surrounded by the symbols of their journey—wooden heart still displayed on the mantel, the carved furniture Noah had built with his own hands, the quilts Emma's mother had made as wedding gifts.

"Your father will be thrilled," Noah said. "And my mother will cry happy tears for a week."

"Everyone will have opinions about names," Emma laughed. "Suggestions about how to raise the baby. Warnings about every possible danger."

"We'll listen politely and then do what we think is

right," Noah replied. "Just like everything else. Honor tradition while finding our own path."

Emma nodded, feeling the truth of that balance they'd fought so hard to achieve. The bakery thrived now, with Emma's innovation section permanently established and drawing customers from neighboring counties. Noah's woodworking business had grown beyond his expectations, with orders for furniture and display pieces coming from both Amish and English customers. He was now working beside Eli Fisher, the friends proving steady business partners.

They'd found a way to honor their heritage while embracing their own gifts, to respect community while maintaining autonomy. It hadn't been easy—there were still whispers, still occasional judgment from those who thought they'd pushed boundaries too far. But mostly, people had come to accept and even celebrate the life they'd built.

"Tell me about the *Englisch* world again," Emma said, settling into Noah's arms. "The cities and the noise and the overwhelming choices."

It had become a kind of ritual between them—Emma asking about Noah's time away, Noah sharing pieces of that experience. Not to glorify it or suggest regret, but to integrate all the parts of his story into their shared life.

"What do you want to know?" Noah asked, his voice soft against her hair.

"What you learned. What you're glad you experienced. What you brought back with you."

Noah considered. "I learned that home isn't a place you're trapped in—it's a place you choose. I learned that sometimes you have to leave to appreciate what you had. I learned that the world is bigger and more diverse than I imagined, but also that the things that matter—love, family, honest work, community—are universal."

"And what did you bring back?"

"Skills, obviously. New techniques, different perspectives. But more than that—I brought back understanding that our way of life is a choice, not a prison. That choosing it deliberately, with eyes open to alternatives, makes it more meaningful than just accepting it because we've never known anything else."

Emma absorbed this, recognizing the truth in his words. She'd never left Miracle Creek physically, but her own journey this past year had been its own kind of departure and return—leaving behind the passive acceptance of others' plans for her life and returning to claim agency over her own choices.

"I'm glad you left," she said finally, surprising herself with the admission. "I hated it at the time, and I wouldn't want to go through that pain again. But if you'd stayed and we'd married young, we'd have been different people. Less tested. Less sure. We needed the separation to become people capable of building something lasting."

"That's very wise," Noah said, a smile in his voice.

"I'm practicing wisdom. Still not very *gut* at it, but I'm trying."

They laughed together, the sound filling their home with warmth and contentment. Outside, snow began falling again, blanketing their small farm—Clover cozy in a warm stable with a new companion, Star.

"Our baby will grow up here," Emma mused, watching snow fall past the window. "Playing in these fields, learning in our church, becoming part of this community."

Noah reached for her hand, his thumb tracing small

circles against her skin. "But also knowing there's a wider world out there," he added. "And that when he or she is old enough, we'll tell them about choices—how their parents each took different roads, but both led back here. That faith isn't about standing still out of fear, but about choosing—eyes open—even in the midst of doubt."

"He or she might choose to leave someday," Emma said, voicing a fear she'd been harboring. "Like you did."

"Maybe. And if they do, we'll trust them to find their way back if this is where they're meant to be. We'll love them through the journey, not just the destination." Noah's hand rested protectively over Emma's belly. "That's the gift our parents eventually gave us—space to choose, patience while we figured things out, welcome when we returned."

Emma thought of Gideon's grudging acceptance that had slowly transformed into genuine pride as Noah proved himself month after month. Of Michael's protective skepticism that had mellowed into brotherly support. Of the bishop's stern warnings that had given way to blessing at their wedding. Of the community that had judged and whispered and eventually celebrated.

"We should finish preparing for tomorrow," Emma said reluctantly, pulling away from Noah's embrace. "There's still so much to do."

"Or," Noah countered, pulling her back, "we could sit by the fire and simply enjoy this moment. The moment we found out we're going to be parents. The moment before we tell everyone and the chaos begins. This quiet, perfect moment that's just ours."

Emma hesitated, then nodded. "You're right. The baking can wait."

They settled by the fire, Emma's head on Noah's

shoulder, his hand resting on her stomach where their child grew. Pippin returned from her exile and curled up on Emma's lap, completing the picture of domestic contentment.

"Tell me what you're thinking," Noah requested after a comfortable silence.

"I'm thinking about gratitude. About how many things had to go right—or go wrong in just the right way—for us to end up here. If you'd never left, if I'd married Isaiah, if the bishop had been less forgiving, if the snowstorm hadn't trapped us in that cabin, if any of a hundred small choices had gone differently—we wouldn't have this."

"Gott working out His perfect plan," Noah said. "The strange way life works when you're brave enough to risk choosing what you really want instead of what feels safe under His hand."

Emma watched flames dance in the fireplace, feeling profoundly grateful for her life in a way she'd never felt before Noah's return had shattered her complacency. "I was so angry when you came back. So hurt and confused and scared."

"I know. You had every right to be."

"But also—somewhere underneath all that—I was relieved. Like part of me had been holding its breath for five years, waiting to see if you'd ever come home. And when you did, even though it was complicated and painful, at least I could finally exhale."

Noah pressed a kiss to the top of her head. "I was terrified you'd moved on completely. That you'd be married to someone else, happy and settled, and I'd have to watch from the outside knowing I'd thrown away the best thing in my life."

"I tried to move on. I really did. But Joanna was right —I never quite managed it. There was always this part of me waiting, hoping, unable to fully commit to any other future because my heart was still caught in our past."

"And now?"

"Now I'm fully here. Fully committed. No part of me waiting for something else." Emma tilted her head to look up at her husband. "You gave me the gift of certainty, Noah. Not by being perfect or by erasing all the hurt, but by staying. By proving day after day that you chose this life, this community, me. That's worth more than any pretty words or romantic gestures."

"I'll keep proving it," Noah promised. "Every day. For you and for our child and for whatever other children we might have."

"Other children?" Emma laughed. "Let's get through this first one."

They sat together as the fire burned low, occasionally adding logs, mostly just existing in companionable silence. Outside, the snow continued its patient work, transforming the landscape one flake at a time.

"I should check on the bread," Emma said eventually, practical concerns reasserting themselves. "Make sure everything's ready for tomorrow."

"I'll help." Noah stood, offering his hand to pull her up. "We're a team now. In everything."

They worked together in the kitchen, Emma organizing ingredients while Noah cleaned dishes and checked her lists. The partnership they'd developed over months of building their life together showed in these small tasks—the way they moved around each other without collision, the way Noah anticipated what Emma needed before she asked, the way Emma trusted him with tasks she'd once insisted on controlling herself.

"This time next year, we'll have a baby at Christmas," Emma mused, mixing dough for tomorrow's bread. "A seven-month-old who'll probably be fussy and disrupting all our carefully planned meals."

"And we'll love every minute of it," Noah replied confidently. "Even the fussy parts."

"You say that now, but wait until you've been up all night with a colicky infant."

"I'll still love it. Because it'll be our colicky infant. Our family. The future we chose together."

Emma's throat tightened with emotion. She'd never felt more blessed, more grateful, more certain that she was exactly where she was meant to be.

***

Christmas morning dawned clear and cold. Emma woke early out of habit, though Noah tried to convince her to stay in bed.

"It's Christmas," he mumbled, pulling her close. "We should sleep in. Be lazy. Scandalous newlyweds ignoring all our duties."

"We have both families coming for dinner. There's still work to do. And Clover and Star need breakfast. Not to mention Pippin." But Emma lingered in his arms for a few more minutes, allowing herself the luxury of starting Christmas Day wrapped in her husband's warmth while Pippin swiped at their feet, urging them to get up.

When they finally rose, they worked together to prepare—Noah building up fires in both the living room and kitchen, Emma organizing food and checking that everything was ready. By the time their families began arriving at noon, the house glowed with warmth and hospitality.

Gideon and Miriam came first, bringing pies and Miriam's famous apple butter. Bethany followed, now sixteen and full of excited chatter about her own courting prospects. Emma noticed the way Noah's father looked around their home with satisfaction, taking in the solid furniture Noah had built, the prosperous feel of a young couple doing well.

"You've done *gut* work here," Gideon said to Noah, the simple words carrying weight of approval that Emma knew meant everything to her husband.

"Thank you, Daed. That means a lot."

The Masts arrived next—Michael and Barbara, Joanna bouncing with her usual enthusiasm. Michael shook Noah's hand firmly, the last remnants of his early skepticism long since transformed into genuine brotherly affection.

"Emma tells me you're expanding the workshop," Michael said as they settled into the living room. "Adding space for apprentices?"

"Thinking about it. There's more demand than I can handle alone, and it would be *gut* to teach the craft to younger boys interested in woodworking." Noah glanced at Emma. "Especially if I'm going to have a son who might want to learn the trade someday."

"Or a daughter," Emma interjected. "Girls can learn woodworking too."

"Or a daughter," Noah agreed, grinning. "Who will undoubtedly be as stubborn about expanding boundaries as her mother."

The families settled into comfortable conversation, the kind that came from growing ease with each other.

Gideon and Michael discussed farming strategies. Miriam and Barbara compared recipes. Bethany and Joanna giggled over some private joke.

And Emma and Noah moved between their guests, hosting together, the partnership they'd built evident in every interaction.

Dinner was abundant—roasted chicken and ham, fresh bread and butter, vegetables from root cellars, pies and cookies and Emma's peppermint bread that had become a holiday tradition. They gathered around the table Noah had built specifically for this purpose, large enough to hold both families with room to spare for future growth.

Bishop Lapp arrived as they were finishing the meal, bringing greetings from the community and a special blessing for their home.

"I wanted to see for myself how our young couple was doing," he said, accepting the coffee Emma offered. "The community is pleased with your success. Both the bakery and the woodworking business reflect well on our commitment to quality and integrity."

"Thank you, Bishop," Noah said. "We're grateful for the community's support."

"You've earned it. Both of you." The bishop's expression softened. "I'll admit, I had doubts when you first returned, Noah. It's not easy for an old man to admit when he's wrong, but I was wrong to be so skeptical. You've proven your commitment many times over."

"I understand your caution. I gave you plenty of reason for it."

"Perhaps. But grace means giving second chances even when they're not earned. You've taught me something about that." The bishop turned to Emma. "And you,

Emma. You've shown courage in following your own judgment even when the community's wisdom suggested a different path. That takes strength of character."

"I had *gut* examples," Emma said, thinking of her grandmother, of Widow Kauffman, of all the women who'd quietly pushed boundaries while maintaining respect for tradition.

After the bishop left, the families lingered into the evening, reluctant to end the celebration. They sang hymns together, shared stories, laughed over memories. As twilight fell, Noah brought out a surprise—a new rocking chair he'd been building in secret, sized perfectly for Emma to nurse their baby when the time came.

"Noah," Emma breathed, running her hands over the smooth wood, the careful joinery, the love evident in every detail. "It's beautiful."

"For you and our child," he said simply. "So you can rock them to sleep and sing them the same songs our mothers sang to us. Keeping the thread going from one generation to the next."

Miriam wiped away tears. Barbara smiled with motherly satisfaction. Even Gideon looked moved, seeing his son fully inhabit the role of husband and soon-to-be father.

As the families prepared to depart, bundling into coats and collecting dishes, Emma stood in the doorway with Noah, watching them load into buggies with promises to gather again soon.

"This is what I dreamed of," Noah said quietly, his arm around Emma's shoulders. "All those years away, this is what I was homesick for. Not just a place but this— family, community, belonging. Being part of something larger than myself."

"And now you have it." Emma leaned into him. "We both do."

After everyone left, they stood together looking at the nativity scene still displayed on the mantel. The Christ child lay in his manger, the face Noah had carved representing hope made tangible.

"Denki," Emma said softly.

"For what?"

"For coming back. For staying. For being brave enough to risk rejection and humble enough to accept correction and faithful enough to keep choosing us every day." She turned to face him fully. "For giving me a future I can be excited about instead of one I'm just resigned to."

"Thank you for waiting. For giving me a second chance I didn't deserve. For seeing who I could become instead of just who I'd been." Noah cupped her face in his hands. "I love you, Emma Mast Albrecht. I loved you when we were teenagers making promises under the stars. I loved you every day I was gone even when I tried not to. And I love you now more than I knew was possible."

"I love you too," Emma whispered. "More than I can find words for."

They kissed in the soft lamplight, Pippin the silent witness to the promise they renewed with each embrace—the promise to keep choosing each other, keep building together, keep honoring the past while creating their future.

Outside, snow began falling again, blanketing their small farm in fresh white. The creek froze solid, waiting for children to skate on it in years to come. The workshop stood ready for tomorrow's work. The garden slept beneath its winter covering, dreaming of spring.

And inside their home, Emma and Noah stood

together, hands joined, two people who'd found their way back to each other through pain and patience and the persistent hope that broken things could be made whole.

Emma's hand rested on her belly where their own child grew, a new generation being woven into the story. She thought of her *Mammi's* recipes, modified and passed down. Of Noah's grandfather's woodworking tools, now in Noah's workshop teaching old skills in new ways. Of all the threads connecting past to present to future, tradition and innovation braided together into something stronger than either alone.

"Merry Christmas," Noah murmured against her hair.

"Merry Christmas, my love."

Outside, the snow continued its patient work. Inside, the fire burned low but steady, warming the home they'd built together—a home founded on forgiveness and faith, on the courage to choose hope over fear, on the revolutionary idea that second chances were real and that broken things, given time and care and love, could be made more beautiful than they'd ever been before.

And in the morning, they'd wake to a new day, a new year stretching ahead full of possibility. They'd tend their businesses, serve their community, prepare for their child. They'd keep choosing each other through ordinary days and extraordinary moments, through challenges and joys, through all the seasons of a life built together.

But tonight, Christmas night, they simply stood in the glow of lamplight and love, grateful beyond words for the journey that had brought them here, ready for whatever came next, together.

The End

Other books in The Miracle Creek series

THE DOCTOR'S AMISH BRIDE (BOOK 1)
She must choose between duty and destiny…

THE AMISH CARPENTER'S HEART (BOOK 2)
She thought her prayers had gone unanswered.
God was just waiting to give her more than she'd dreamed."

HEARTS IN THE SNOW (BOOK 3)
He left the Amish world years ago… This Christmas, he's
coming home—for the woman he never forgot.

THE OTHER AMISH GIRL (BOOK 4)
Some hearts are stitched together by a single misunderstood
word… and only the truth can unpick the past.

BENEATH THE CHRISTMAS STARS (BOOK 5)
In the hush of snow and starlight,
two hearts find their way home.

THE AMISH TEACHER'S LESSON IN LOVE (BOOK 6)
She teaches children. He guards his heart.
Can love find a way through grief and fear?

THE AMISH LOCKSMITH'S KEY TO HER HEART (BOOK 7)
Some keys don't just open doors. They open the way to love.

THE AMISH FARMER'S PROMISE (BOOK 8)
In the quiet fields of Miracle Creek,
two souls tend the same dream.

And more to come!